"I think you'd better back off, Henderson,"

Molly announced.

"Not this time, Duncan," Sam shot back.

"Excuse me?"

"I backed off last night. I'm not retreating again."

She folded her arms across her chest. "You're treading shaky ground here, Major. Get something straight. I left Boston to get away from a man who tried to dictate my choices. I don't need another one trying the same thing here."

"So what are you going to do if I press you too hard or too soon, sweetheart?" Sam answered. "Run away again?"

Molly tilted her head back. In his eyes she saw a fierceness that skidded right past lust into a feeling that made her heart trip. Her anger dissipated, and in its place came an answering emotion so strong that she didn't try to fight it anymore.

"No, Sam," she said at last. "I'm not running away. This time I'm standing my ground."

Dear Reader,

The kids are on their way back to school, and that means more time for this month's fabulous Intimate Moments novels. Leading the way is Beverly Barton, with *Lone Wolf's Lady,* sporting our WAY OUT WEST flash. This is a steamy story about Luke McClendon's desire to seduce Deanna Atchley and then abandon her, as he believes she abandoned him years ago. But you know what they say about best-laid plans....

You also won't want to miss Merline Lovelace's *If a Man Answers.* A handsome neighbor, a misdialed phone call...an unlikely path to romance, but you'll love going along for the ride. Then check out Linda Randall Wisdom's *A Stranger Is Watching,* before welcoming Elizabeth August to the line. *Girls' Night Out* is also one of our MEN IN BLUE titles, with an irresistible cop as the hero. Our WHOSE CHILD? flash adorns Terese Ramin's wonderful *Mary's Child.* Then finish up the month with Kylie Brant's *Undercover Lover,* about best friends becoming something more.

And when you've finished, mark your calendar for next month, when we'll be offering you six more examples of the most exciting romances around—only in Silhouette Intimate Moments.

Yours,

[signature]

Leslie J. Wainger
Executive Senior Editor

Please address questions and book requests to:
Silhouette Reader Service
U.S.: 3010 Walden Ave., P.O. Box 1325, Buffalo, NY 14269
Canadian: P.O. Box 609, Fort Erie, Ont. L2A 5X3

IF A MAN ANSWERS

MERLINE LOVELACE

Silhouette®
INTIMATE™MOMENTS®

Published by Silhouette Books

America's Publisher of Contemporary Romance

SILHOUETTE BOOKS

ISBN 0-373-07878-1

IF A MAN ANSWERS

This edition published by arrangement with Harlequin Books S.A.

® and TM are trademarks of Harlequin Books S.A., used under license. Trademarks indicated with ® are registered in the United States Patent and Trademark Office, the Canadian Trade Marks Office and in other countries.

Printed in U.S.A.

MERLINE LOVELACE

served tours of duty in Vietnam, at the Pentagon and at bases all over the world as a career air force officer. In the process, she stored up enough adventures to keep her fingers flying over the keyboards for years to come. When not glued to her computer, Merline loves to travel with Al, her own handsome hero and husband of twenty-seven years, and chase little white balls around the golf courses of Oklahoma.

Watch for Merline's next books: *A Drop of Frankincense,* part of the Harlequin Historicals 1998 Christmas anthology, and *The Mercenary and the New Mom,* the conclusion of the exciting FOLLOW THAT BABY cross-line miniseries, coming from Silhouette Intimate Moments in February 1999.

Merline enjoys hearing from readers and can be reached at P.O. Box 892717, Oklahoma City, OK, 73189.

Chapter 1

"Dammit! Doesn't the blasted man *ever* sleep?"

Yanking her pillow out from under her neck, Molly Duncan mashed it down over her head. Even with both ears covered, she still couldn't shut out the nasal lament that drifted across the desert night from the house next door.

She despised country music. She despised dragging herself out of bed after groggy, sleepless nights. She was fast coming to despise her new neighbor.

Until Sam Henderson had moved into the house next to hers, Molly had thoroughly enjoyed her life in Las Vegas. She'd moved to Nevada only six months ago, after dumping a fiancé more into control than her independent spirit could tolerate. Eagerly, she'd traded cold, wet Boston winters for the year-round desert sunshine and a position as a translator and tour consultant for the Las Vegas Trade and Convention Center. From the moment she'd crested the hills and driven down into the sparkling jewel that was Vegas, she'd reveled in its gaudy glitz. Buying her very first home had been the icing on the cake of her new life.

Then, just a few weeks ago, the Major had moved in next door.

She'd received several letters addressed to him in her mailbox by mistake, so Molly knew he was a retired Air Force major…a major pain in the bohunkus, in her considered opinion. She couldn't believe how swiftly their initial skirmish over a dented garbage can had escalated into an undeclared war.

And she'd never even spoken a word to the man!

Okay, so maybe the note she taped to his trash can the morning she ran over it, requesting that he keep the darned thing on his side of their parallel driveways, was a bit, well, unneighborly. But she was late for work, and picking up someone else's smelly garbage wasn't exactly her idea of a fun way to start the day.

Still, that was no reason for Henderson to fire a broadside in return. Even now, the memory of the note she'd found shoved under her front door that same night steamed her. The terse missive had assured Ms. Duncan that he'd keep his trash can in a safe, no-fire zone. In return, she might consider taking a few driving lessons. Judging by the ruts she dug in the lava rock between their driveways when she squealed out of the garage each morning, she could use them. Or maybe she was just feeling the aftereffects of the several cases of empty beer cans he'd observed in *her* recycling bin?

Molly didn't dignify the obnoxious note with a reply. The fact that she slathered a beer-based facial across her nose and cheeks every night to keep her splatter of freckles under control was no one's business but hers. She did, however, respond to the notice she received from Henderson a few days later, informing her that the oleander hedge she'd planted for privacy when she first moved in was actually three feet beyond her property line. According to the contractor hired by Major Sam Henderson, the hedge would have to come down to accommodate the pool he wanted to put in his backyard. The hedge's fate, Molly had replied in a scathing letter to the contractor, would be decided by the county surveyor's office.

She humped the pillow over her ears, furious all over again at the thought of anyone wanting to tear up the row of beautiful hot pink oleanders she'd put in with her own hands. The nerve of the man!

It was just her luck that her new neighbor's personality didn't live up to his admittedly gorgeous physique. In the past few weeks, Molly had caught a few glimpses of the reclusive Major, stripped to the waist and poking around under the hood of a classic, flame-colored Mustang convertible. She had to admit that he possessed a set of world-class buns. And, yes, his glistening, sweaty pecs had pretty well closed down her respiratory system. Based on those gorgeous muscles alone, she might have called a truce in their war and learned to peacefully coexist if Sam Henderson's damned nocturnal habits hadn't destroyed all hope of a cease-fire.

A morning person, Molly always faded fast when the sun went down. Her neighbor, she'd decided soon after he moved in, was part vampire. If he ever slept, she didn't know when. The soul-searing country music he listened to hour after hour seemed to drone on all night. Every night. She'd put up with it as long as she could, but finally had to protest.

The first time she'd called to complain, a sultry-voiced female promised to give Sam the message…when he got out of the shower.

The second time, she'd let the phone ring and ring with no answer.

This time, she vowed, dragging her head out from under the pillow, she meant business!

She glanced at the clock radio sitting atop the overturned cardboard box she used as a nightstand and groaned. Ten after one, for heaven's sake, and she was scheduled to meet a delegation of Japanese businessmen for breakfast at seven.

Shoving her flyaway blond hair out of her eyes, she sat up and rummaged around in the scatter of papers on the box for the envelope she'd written her neighbor's number on. The scribbled digits blurred a bit, probably from the wet glass she'd left on top of the envelope. Tilting it to a different angle, she reached for the receiver. Seven quick punches and the phone started to ring.

Tapping her bare toes on the smooth oak floor-boards, Molly marshaled her thoughts. She refused, absolutely refused, to allow another husky-voiced female to fob her off. This time she'd insist on speaking to the Major himself…even if she had to march next door and confront him in person.

She didn't have to march anywhere. A man answered on the third ring.

"Yeah?"

Molly blinked, surprised by the distinctive twang in the single syllable. Her trained ear placed the accent immediately. New Jersey. Possibly lower New York, but most likely upper Jersey.

Based on his choice in music and worn, low-heeled cowboy boots, Molly had assumed Henderson hailed from somewhere west of the Hudson River. Not that she cared *where* the man came from as long as he lowered the volume on his blasted CD player.

"This is Molly Duncan, next door. Would you *please* turn down that…"

A doorbell shrilled in the background. Unceremoniously, her neighbor cut her off.

"Hang on. There's someone at the door."

"Wait a minute! I just want you to…."

"Hold the phone, doll."

The receiver dropped onto a hard surface. Molly winced at the loud clatter, then scowled at the framed poster of Las Vegas by night on her whitewashed walls. Crossing one knee over the other, she swung her leg impatiently. Another sad lament drifted through her window, telling the story of a trucker who lost his wife to a city boy.

She wished she could lose her neighbor. In fact, she wished she could lose him, his music, his confounded garbage cans, his....

"Don't shoot! God, don't shoot!"

The hoarse cry ripped like a jagged knife through her rambling thoughts. She jerked upright, her jaw dropping. What the heck?

"I have to," a soft, cultured voice replied. "Surely you understand why."

Upper Midwestern, Molly catalogued without conscious thought. Wisconsin, most likely.

"No! No! I won't say nuthin', I swear!"

She'd just decided that the dramatic dialogue had to be emanating from some B-grade movie on her neighbor's TV when she heard a queer little pop. An agonized, gurgling shriek. Another pop. A thud.

Then only silence.

Frozen with disbelief, Molly gripped the phone.

It had to be the TV! Surely that desperate plea hadn't come from her neighbor! Surely those weren't real shots she'd just heard!

She strained, listening for something more. Anything. A bit of dialogue. A dramatic surge of background music to indicate the TV show had just reached a climax.

After what seemed like an eternity, someone picked up the receiver. Quietly. Deliberately.

"Hello?"

Molly's throat closed.

Good grief! This was no movie. The same soft, cultured voice she'd heard a moment ago was now speaking directly to her. She couldn't reply. Couldn't force so much as a squeak through her frozen vocal chords.

Silence descended once more. The person at the other end of the line listened. Just listened.

Like an animal suddenly sensing danger, Molly slammed the receiver down. Her heart hammered. Her whole body shook in a delayed reaction. Trembling violently, she stabbed at the phone buttons once again.

"Hello, 911," a Hispanic female replied with practiced calm. "What is your emergency?"

"A shooting! There's been a shooting!"

The woman's voice took on a sharper edge. "Have you been shot?"

"No! No, I…uh…my neighbor…."

"You shot your neighbor?"

This wasn't the time for Molly to admit that she'd thought about it. More than once.

"No, I heard someone shoot him. Over the phone. The doorbell rang. My neighbor shouted a protest, and then I heard shots. You have to send someone right away. Whoever fired them is still in his house!"

"I have your name and address on my screen. Are you Ms. Duncan?"

"Yes!"

"Please confirm your neighbor's address?"

"Uh…sixty-seven-nineteen…No, sixty-seven-twenty-one South Valley. I think."

She threw a frantic glance at the curtained windows, trying to get her bearings. The mountains were behind her house. The interstate just a couple of miles away ran north and south.

"His house is to the north of mine. At the end of the cul-de-sac."

"Please hold on the line while I dispatch the police, Ms. Duncan."

The operator came back a moment later, her voice once more calm and steady.

"There's a squad car only a few blocks away. They're on their way. Are you by yourself?"

"Yes."

"Are you safe? Do you feel threatened?"

"Nooo...."

Just scared to death, she thought with a shiver.

"Please stay away from the windows and remain on the line. Can you give me any more information that might aid the police when they arrive?"

While Molly added what little she could to the details she'd already provided, she couldn't help picturing the scene next door. Her neighbor might be lying in a pool of blood. His life might be seeping away second by second. Oh, God! He might already be dead. Waves of guilt for all the awful things she'd wished on Sam Henderson came crashing down on her.

"Ms. Duncan?"

"Maybe I should do something. Try to help him."

"No!"

"He could be dying. Bleeding to death."

"Ms. Duncan, listen to me. The last thing we need is for you to go next door and put yourself in danger. Please, just remain on the line until the police arrive at the scene."

"Yes, but…"

She searched her bedroom for a weapon. The most lethal object she could spot was a tennis racket she'd been intending to take in for restringing. Maybe she could sneak through the oleander hedge and lob the racket through her neighbor's window. Set off his alarm. Scare the shooter away.

The realization that she might also scare herself right into the line of fire of a cold-blooded killer added another kink to the knot in Molly's stomach. Suddenly, a siren wailed in the distance. She heaved a ragged sigh of relief.

"Thank God! I hear the police."

"Stay put until they contact you."

The tennis racket forgotten, Molly mumbled an assent and hung up. Her bare feet slapped the oak floor as she hurried down the hall to the upstairs front bedroom. Lifting the shade aside a few inches, she watched two black-and-white patrol cars pull into her neighbor's drive. Weapons drawn and angled at the night sky, they approached the red-roofed, stucco house. After peering in the darkened front windows, one officer skirted the garage and headed for the back. The other disappeared into the shadows on the far side of the house.

Molly had no idea how long she crouched there in the front bedroom, her nerves crawling. It felt like hours. To her mingled relief and consternation, nothing happened. No gunfire shattered the night. No shouts sounded from the house or yard. No ambulances pulled into the driveway, sirens flashing.

Finally, the officers returned to the front. From where she crouched, Molly couldn't see whether they kicked in the door or found it unlocked. In any case, an oblong of yellow light slashed through the darkness.

Shivering, she let the shade fall. Whatever the police found next door, she'd better get dressed. The operator had said they'd want to talk to her.

Her doorbell sounded just as she was splashing away the remnants of her facial. Hastily, she swiped a towel over her face and pulled on a soft gray cotton top and leggings. The wide-necked tunic slipped off one shoulder as she hurried on down the stairs and into the hall that led to the tiled front entryway.

Scrunching one eye shut, she peered through the peephole with the other. At the glint of a silver metal shield prominently displayed on a dark-shirted chest, she yanked off the chain, twisted the dead bolt, and threw open the door.

"Ms. Duncan?"

"Yes!"

"I'm Officer Dennis Rodriguez. My backup, Officer Corrigan, is in his patrol car, notifying central dispatch."

"Thank God you got here so quickly. What did you find next door?"

"He found me, Ms. Duncan," a deep voice snarled. "Alive, unshot, and, at this point, thoroughly ticked off by your stupid stunt."

Molly jerked back, startled by the half-naked male who stepped forward to confront her. Unsnapped jeans rode low on his hips. A white towel dangled around his neck. Sweat glistened on his heavily muscled torso.

Her nerves snapping like live electrical wires, Molly dragged her stunned gaze from that acre or so of smooth, muscled chest to the face that went with it. Too rugged for handsomeness, too square-jawed for charm, it was the kind of face that would make any woman back up a step, even when it wasn't tight with anger...which at this point, it definitely was! Below a thick pelt of sweat-slicked hair so dark a brown it looked black in this light, his slanting brows slashed to a *V*. Slate gray eyes lasered into Molly.

"Is this your idea of a joke?" he demanded in a scorching drawl.

No trace of New Jersey there, she thought, torn between relief and confusion. Her neighbor definitely hailed from west of the Hudson. Somewhere in the Southwest, she thought. Arizona, or maybe he was one of that rare genus, a Nevada native.

Obviously, this wasn't the man who answered her call a while ago. Frowning, she responded to his irate demand.

"No, of course it isn't a joke."

His big fists gripped the ends of the towel, knuckles white. "If you insist on continuing this damned feud you started, you should at least have the guts to do it in person."

"The feud *I* started?" Molly practically sputtered with indignation. "Let's get something straight here. I wasn't the one who put my garbage cans smack in the middle of someone else's driveway. Nor was I pulling some stupid stunt when I called the police tonight. I heard shots and thought you'd been wounded or killed. Next time," she promised darkly, "I won't bother to report it."

"Next time," her neighbor fired back, "you might consider laying off the beer and maybe you won't hear strange noises in your head."

Hastily, the uniformed police officer intervened.

"Could we take this inside, folks? I need to ask Ms. Duncan a few questions."

Tight-lipped, she led the way down the tiled entry hall to the archway that opened onto the living area. A flick of a wall switch bathed the high-ceilinged, open-beamed room in soft, recessed light. It also illuminated the fact that the room's furnishings consisted of a single rattan chair cushioned in cool desert mauves, a gnarled cypress stump that did duty as an end table, and a scattering of oversized pillows.

When she'd walked away from her ex-fiancé, Molly had subleased her Boston co-op fully furnished. Eager for a new beginning in Vegas, she'd emptied her bank account to make the down payment on this house. She'd almost saved up enough to splurge on the leather sectional sofa and chair she had her eye on. After that, she intended to work on a table and chairs for the dining room. Right now, though, she made do with cardboard boxes, gnarled tree stumps and a tall stool pulled up to the kitchen counter.

With a wave of one hand, she gave the two men a choice of chair or pillow. Both opted to stand. Officer Rodriguez pulled out a notebook and pen.

"Will you tell me exactly what you heard, Ms. Duncan?"

"I heard the most god-awful wailing coming from next door," she replied with a searing glance at her neighbor. "I've been hearing it for the past two or three hours."

The Major appeared taken aback for a moment, then his scowl deepened. "I take it you're referring to my Buck Randall CDs?"

"If that's who's putting out that tinny, wheezing noise night after night, yes."

Henderson shook his head in disgust. Even Rodriguez looked faintly disapproving. Obviously, this country crooner was a local favorite.

"If my music's been bothering you, why the hell didn't you call and let me know?"

"I did," Molly retorted, her Boston-Irish temper up. "Twice. The first time, some whipped cream and chocolate-voiced woman promised to pass you my message. The second time, no one answered the phone. Why don't you get an answering machine?" she muttered irritably.

"Right. So you can leave obnoxious messages on

it about my garbage cans instead of taping them to my front door?''

Refusing to respond to that deliberate provocation, Molly continued. ''After listening to this Boots Randolph…''

''Buck Randall,'' the two men chorused.

''…Buck Randall for two agonizing hours, I got up, turned on the light and dialed Major Henderson's number. A man answered.'' She jerked her head at her neighbor. ''I thought it was him.''

''And then what happened?''

She ran through the sequence of events, shivering a bit when she got to the part about the eerie silence after the shooting.

''Is it possible that you dialed the wrong number?'' Rodriguez asked when she finished.

''Yes, it's possible,'' she admitted, having already come to that conclusion herself. ''The numbers were a bit blurry.''

''Why am I not surprised?'' the Major said with a little snort. ''You put out more empties in the morning than a waterfront dive. And that's not chicken soup I smell coming from the kitchen.''

What he smelled was her grandmother's recipe for beer-bran mush. Molly had brewed up a fresh batch earlier this evening, but she was damned if she was going to explain that fact to Major Sam Henderson. Her jaw tight, she finished her report.

''Then I dialed 911 and reported what I thought was a shooting.''

''Well, if there was a shooting, it didn't occur at

Major Henderson's residence,'' Rodriguez concluded, stating the obvious.

"There was a shooting,'' Molly insisted. "I heard it.''

The police officer flipped his notebook shut. "We'll get the phone company to verify the number you dialed and make a few calls of our own, just to see who or what turns up.''

Molly started to point out that dead persons don't answer the phone, but kept her mouth shut. She was already beginning to feel more like the perpetrator of a hoax than the reporter of a possible crime.

Rodriguez headed for the entryway. "It could have been kids. Pulling a late-night prank.''

She followed more slowly, shaking her head. "Those weren't kids I heard.''

"Well, if we find out anything, we'll let you know.''

"Please do. It was so real.'' As balmy as it was, the desert air raised a chill on her arms. "So frightening.''

Nodding, the police officer headed for the black-and-white squad car. The Major followed him out, but turned halfway down the paved walk. He searched Molly's face, his own cast in shadows.

"Look, I'm sorry about the music.''

The gruff apology surprised her. After the way he'd all but called her a drunk, however, Molly wasn't about to accept it with any degree of graciousness.

"You should be.''

"I didn't realize the sound carried so clearly across our yards...and I didn't get your previous message."

His tone implied that he had doubts she'd ever left it. Molly bristled all over again.

"I'll keep the volume turned down in the future."

"Thank you."

Curling his hands around the towel ends, he studied her a moment longer. "You all right?"

The reluctance behind the question came through loud and clear. Obviously, he didn't want to get involved with someone he considered a drunk or a neurotic, at the very least.

"No," Molly replied acidly, "As a matter of fact, I'm not all right. I'm tired, I have an early appointment in the morning, and I just heard someone get shot...I think," she finished on a mutter.

By this time, she wasn't quite sure what she'd heard. All she wanted to do was to climb back into bed, pull the covers over her head and try to blank this whole, nightmarish incident from her mind.

With a curt good-night, she turned and slammed the door.

Sam walked barefooted across the concrete driveways that divided the front of his property from that of his prickly, pesky neighbor.

The headache he'd been trying to drive out of his mind with a punishing workout before the cops had pounded on his door had now doubled in intensity. Instead of lancing through the back of his head with knife-like precision, the damned thing roared around in his skull like a high performance jet in full thrust.

Damn! As if ejecting helmet-first through a malfunctioning aircraft canopy and being placed on a temporary disability retirement list weren't bad enough. Now, just when he needed time and space and quiet to figure out what the hell he was going to do if the medical evaluation board put him out to pasture permanently, he had to move in next door to a beer-guzzling wacko.

He still couldn't quite buy her story about hearing a shooting. It wouldn't surprise him if she'd called the cops just to harass him. She'd been on his case since the day he moved in, starting with her snippy note about the garbage can, then threatening to take him to court over her weedy bushes...which she'd planted on *his* property, for Pete's sake!

No doubt about it. Despite those mile-long legs and flashing green eyes, the woman was trouble.

Too bad. In another time, or with another woman, he might have found a way to satisfy this crazy urge to rake his fingers through that tumble of wheat-colored, shoulder-length hair. Or maybe tasted that sulky mouth, which might have been luscious if she hadn't kept it all tight and unsmiling. He certainly would have teased a smile into those green eyes that went from nervous to indignant to confused as the interview progressed. Of course, Sam thought with a snort, all those Coors she'd been tipping might have something to do with that haze of confusion.

She hadn't sounded drunk, though. Hadn't acted it, either.

Frowning, he slammed his front door and twisted the dead bolt. Maybe the woman *had* heard a shooting. Or what someone wanted her to think was a shooting. Maybe she'd really called the police to come to his rescue, instead of sending them to his door to harass him, as he'd first assumed.

He shook his head at the memory of his less than appreciative response, then winced as the abrupt movement sent fingers of white-hot fire from one side of his skull to the other.

Dammit, he'd sort it all out tomorrow. Maybe even apologize to his neighbor…and mean it this time. Someone had to call a truce in the ridiculous war that had sprung up between them. First, though, he had to get through the rest of the night.

Mindful of her acid comment about his choice in music, Sam crossed to the built-in bookshelves that took up one wall of his great room and turned down the volume on the CD player. Buck Randall's tribute to the night dropped to a ribbon of mournful sound.

He tossed his towel at the couch shoved up against the wall to make room for the universal gym he had installed shortly after he moved in. His feet sinking into the protective rubber pad under the steel structure, he stretched out on the narrow bench. He grasped the handlebar, grunted, and slowly worked his way back into the rhythm of the punishing routine the police had interrupted. It took a while, but eventually the intense strain on his body blanked both the pain and the tantalizing image of his neighbor from his head.

He finished his workout an hour later, then showered and prowled the house for a while before hitting the sack. He dozed off just before dawn, only to awaken to the sound of tires squealing down the driveway next door. Sam winced, thinking of the new ruts he'd find in the tiny strip of desert landscape that separated his drive from his neighbor's.

He'd better forget about trying to effect a truce, he told himself wryly. Forget about going next door with another apology. The less he had to do with the ditzy, tumble-haired Ms. Molly Duncan, the better. He didn't need to complicate his life any further with the kind of baggage she carted around with her.

He finally drifted off to sleep, unaware that his ditzy, tumble-haired neighbor would come crashing through her damned oleanders that very night and throw herself and a whole bagful of complications right into Sam's arms.

Chapter 2

Molly's Tuesday morning started off bad and went downhill from there. After tossing and turning for what was left of the night, she hit the snooze button on the clock radio a few too many times. Full consciousness didn't occur until a newscaster came on and finally broke through her grogginess. She listened to his patter for a few drowsy seconds until he announced the time. Jerking her head out of the pillow, she stared at the clock in disbelief.

''Six-thirty! Oh, no!''

Throwing off the covers, Molly dashed to the bathroom and splashed cold water on her face. Thankfully, her honey blond, shoulder-length waves didn't require anything more than a quick run through with a brush and a hand-scrunch or two. She slapped on a matte foundation to cover her freckles and protect her skin from the fierce Nevada sun, dabbed a mascara wand at her lashes, swiped on some lipstick and spun out of the bathroom.

After a quick search of her closet, she pulled on strappy black sandals and yanked a silky chiffon black-and-white polka-dot dress off the hanger. Tying the sash on the run, she snatched up a black scarf and her purse and raced out of the bedroom. Downstairs, she threw a look of intense longing at the coffeepot on her way to the garage. She had no time for coffee. No time for anything if she was going to make her seven o'clock meeting with the president of Sato Motors International.

Early September heat already shimmered above the concrete as Molly shoved her car key in the ignition. With a twist of the ignition key, she squealed out of the garage and peeled down the drive. In the process, she took the curve onto the cul-de-sac a bit too wide. The tires threw up a spray of lava rock from the landscaped area that separated her drive from the Major's.

Wincing, Molly flicked a quick glance at her neighbor's house. The shades were drawn, thank goodness, and the place showed no signs of life. After snide cracks Sam Henderson had made about her driving last night, she hated to hand him any more ammunition to use in their continuing battle.

Although…

For a moment there, Molly had sensed a slight lessening of hostilities. She had to admit that his apology had surprised her. Okay, everything about the man surprised her, from his nocturnal habits to his gruff personality. What a shame that a bod like his was wasted on someone with such a touchy disposition.

A mental image formed of the Major as she'd last seen him, bathed in streetlight, muscles gleaming, jeans riding low on his hips. At the memory of his raw maleness, an unexpected dart of heat arrowed right through Molly's stomach. Startled, she dug her nails into the leather-wrapped steering wheel. It took a conscious effort of will to relax them.

For heaven's sake, she didn't even like the man! If he continued in his pigheaded determination to dig up his whole backyard...and her bushes with it... they might well end up in court. She had no business imagining what his rugged face would look like without that tight scowl, or recalling the dark hair that swirled down his stomach to disappear inside his jeans. Shaking her head to dislodge the persistent image, Molly concentrated on zigzagging down the hill that led from her housing development.

The open stretch of road at the bottom of the hill tempted her to nudge the speed limit just a bit. The flat desert landscape wouldn't remain empty for long, Molly saw with a twinge of regret. Already huge round concrete culverts lined either side of the road, waiting to be buried. The steel girders of a new high school rose from the desert floor. With a fleeting regret for the loss of this stretch of wild, desolate beauty, she whizzed past saguaro cacti and silvery tumbleweeds.

Fourteen minutes later, her little white Trans Am convertible screeched to a halt at the pillared entrance to the Addagio, the Strip's newest and most expensive resort and casino. Re-created to look like a fourteenth-century Venetian palazzo, the complex covered several city blocks. Tossing the keys to the parking valet, Molly hurried through a lobby filled with replicas of gorgeous antiques and glittering neon. After confirming her appointment with the concierge, she stepped into a private elevator that accessed the penthouse suite. The elegant, paneled cage whirred her upward.

A quick peek at her watch had her sagging against the wall in relief. She'd made it, with two minutes to spare! A few quick jabs with her fingers restored her hair to a casual disorder. Several deep, calming breaths restored her poise.

Mr. Sato and his entourage were waiting for her in the magnificent suite. The sitting room alone contained more square footage than the entire downstairs of Molly's house. Even more spectacular was the 270-degree view of Las Vegas and the surrounding mountains in early morning sunlight. The view at night, she knew from previous visits, had to be seen to be believed.

The men rose at her entrance. Smiling, she greeted Mr. Sato in fluent Japanese, then switched to English for the benefit of the hotel's vice president for sales.

"I see you're ready to begin your presentation, Mr. Hamilton."

"As soon as we finish breakfast, Ms. Duncan. Would you care to sample the buffet?"

Molly's stomach somersaulted in delight as she took a quick trip into the dining room. The Addagio had pulled out all stops in its effort to impress Mr. Sato and company. They certainly impressed her. The artfully presented array of hot and cold dishes constituted a major test of her willpower. With real regret, she limited herself to just two of the mouth-watering pastries, a plate of fruit and the most delicious sushi she'd ever eaten. She'd developed a taste for the cold rice cakes during her junior year in college, which she'd spent in an exchange program at the University of Tokyo.

As soon as the attentive wait staff had cleared the dishes and refilled everyone's cups, Mr. Hamilton began his presentation. Without seeming too eager, the sales director made it clear that the Addagio wanted to host Sato Motors International's annual convention for the year 2001. They were well aware of the millions that SMI's well-paid employees would drop in the casino before, during and after their convention.

Although most of the Sato executives spoke and read English, Molly was on hand to interpret, if necessary. She would also escort Mr. Sato and his staff to the various sites they wanted to scout in the area. Unfortunately, the visiting CEO had somehow formed the mistaken impression that her duties extended to more than escorting and interpreting. On the first morning of his visit, Mr. Sato had offered

Molly a staggering sum in exchange for her exclusive companionship at night. She'd politely refused. Since then, she'd discovered that he had difficulty understanding "no" in either Japanese or English.

Twice during the Addagio's long presentation, she removed his pudgy fingers from her thigh. The second time, she pinned a bright smile on her face and let him know in a private aside that she'd send him home to his wife in two separate suitcases if he touched her again.

After grinding out a polite farewell, Molly finally left Mr. Sato and his group to a night of gambling and whatever debauchery they cared to seek out. She also left a sublimely happy vice president of sales hugging a signed contract to his Versace-clad chest. Worn out by her long day and even longer night, she drove to the Las Vegas Convention and Visitors Authority just off Paradise Road. Her boss had asked for a full report. As expected, Davinia Jacobbson whooped with joy at the news that Sato had signed with the Addagio.

"That means some ten thousand Sato employees will descend on the city, along with their families and assorted friends. Good goin', kiddo."

Her infectious delight pulled a grin from Molly. A former college student turned showgirl turned entertainment attorney, Davinia still flashed long legs and a ten-megawatt smile. Now director of convention management, she had recently shucked her third husband and was actively auditioning candidate number four.

"This calls for a celebration," she exclaimed. "The Center's got some tickets for the big fight at the arena tonight." She waggled eyebrows a shade or two darker than her gloriously platinum hair. "Want to go watch while two hunks of superb maleness pound each other into a bloody pulp?"

"No thanks," Molly replied, laughing. "I'm too pooped for pulp."

Davinia shook her head in despair. "Good golly, Miss Molly, we have to find something or someone who can keep you awake after the sun goes down. Vegas doesn't fizz to life until midnight."

"Vegas might fizz to life, but I fizzle out. Besides, I had a long night last night."

"Oh?" Davinia's face brightened with interest. "Don't tell me you actually lived it up for once."

"I wouldn't call spending half of the night listening to some honky-tonk cowboy with seriously overdeveloped adenoids named Boots Randall and the other half with the police living it up."

"If you mean Buck Randall," Davinia drawled, "he and his adenoids are headlining at Caesars next week. But what's this about the cops?"

"Well, you know the running war I've been having with my neighbor...."

"The phantom of the night?" She bristled on her employee's behalf. "Has that jerk been hassling you again?"

"Well...."

"I wish you'd let me turn ex-number-two loose on him. John's a total pig most of the time, I'll admit, but he aced property law and civil torts when we were in law school together. He'll tie your creep of a neighbor into so many legal knots, the man won't know his backyard from his backside."

Molly smiled at the tempting offer, but declined. "There's no need to loose number two just yet. The Major didn't exactly hassle me, except with his taste in music. And I did a bit of hassling in return."

Briefly, she recounted the previous night's events. Davinia's eyes rounded as Molly described her disturbing phone call, the police response, and her neighbor's half-naked and wholly irate appearance on her doorstep shortly afterward.

"The police officer who came out to the house promised to get a record of my outgoing calls from the phone company," Molly finished. "He said he'd let me know if he found anything."

"You'd better check your voice mail," Davinia advised, frowning. "Your calls have been piling up all day."

With her boss trailing behind her, Molly headed for her office.

The sleek glass cubicle contained less than half the square footage of her Boston office, but Molly didn't mind. She wasn't hung up on the trappings of power or the latest in modular office equipment. The wide-ranging scope of her new job and the excitement of living in Las Vegas more than made up for the smaller digs.

Skirting the walnut console, she punched the play button on her phone. Sure enough, one of the recorded messages was from Dennis Rodriguez. The phone company computers had experienced some kind of glitch, he reported. He hadn't been able to get the information he'd requested. He'd call back when he did.

Molly wavered between disappointment and relief. Part of her had hoped that the police could trace the call and verify what she'd heard last night. Another part was willing to be convinced that she'd imagined the whole thing.

"I'm going home," she announced, pushing her chair back. "After what I went through last night and with Mr. Sato today, all I want is a cool glass of wine, a hot bath and a night of blissful, uninterrupted sleep."

She managed only one out of the three.

As she drove home, the beauty of the desert landscape went a long way to soothing her frazzled nerves. With the approach of dusk, the hundred-degree-plus heat of the day had softened to a balmy eighty-five or so. The warm air rippled like silk against her skin. Even the dust thrown onto the road by the bulldozers digging trenches for the massive concrete culverts caused only a momentary annoyance as she sped by. She soon left the dust behind and took the winding road that led to the houses tucked in the rolling foothills.

When she swung the wheel to turn into her driveway, the city shimmered in the rearview mirror. Molly drank in the spectacular sight while the garage door rumbled up. Even at its gaudiest, Vegas had its own unique beauty.

Feeling relaxed for the first time all day, she sent the door rumbling down again and went inside. Her home welcomed her with a graciousness that still gave her a thrill after six months. Even the empty spaces seemed elegantly spare, not stark and uninviting.

Tossing her purse on the kitchen counter, she revised her planned agenda. She'd indulge in a long, hot shower first. Then pour herself a relaxing glass of wine. Then, if her neighbor stuck to his promise to keep Boots/Buck to a low wail, she'd sink into blissful oblivion.

She went upstairs, shedding her dress, shoes and underwear in careless abandon as she crossed her bedroom. She wasn't a messy person by nature, but there was something to be said for the freedom of picking up when and where the mood struck her. A quick twist of the faucet soon steamed the shower. With a sigh of contentment, Molly stepped inside.

When she finally flipped off the pulsing jets, she felt as limp as overcooked linguini. Pulling on a pair of purple satin boxer shorts and her favorite midriff-baring University of Syracuse T-shirt, she towel dried her hair. Under the glare of the bathroom lights, she slathered several generous dollops of fresh-brewed facial across her nose and upper cheeks.

The beer-bran mush tightened her pores with a satisfying tingle. As she knew from long experience, the home-brewed facial would also keep her splatter of freckles from multiplying like busy little rabbits while she slept. The downside, of course, was that the concoction dried to a tight mask and flaked all over her pillow during the night. That was a minor inconvenience, in Molly's considered opinion. Her grandmother still turned heads at seventy-eight, and a complexion like Rose Duncan's was worth a few flakes on the pillow.

Brady hadn't agreed, of course, but that was only one of Molly's personal quirks her former fiancé had begun to criticize. When he'd started in on her friends, her taste in clothes, and even her decision to splurge on the little white Trans Am instead of the yuppie four-wheel-drive Explorer he thought they should have, Molly had finally rebelled. The ensuing argument had *not* been pretty, but the angry, hurtful confrontation had led to her new life and her new house.

Wondering why in the world she'd put up with her overly controlling ex-fiancé as long as she had, Molly headed downstairs for her long-anticipated glass of wine. She'd just poured her favorite California blush into a stemmed glass and lifted it for a taste when she heard a thump in the living room.

Startled, she jerked around. In the process, she splashed most of the wine down her front. The soft cotton soaked up the chilled liquid like a sponge. Molly in turn soaked up the sound of quiet footsteps in the hallway leading to the kitchen.

She froze, eyes wide and staring at the dimly lit hall. When she spotted what looked like a shadow moving toward the kitchen, Molly did what any reasonably intelligent, semi-intrepid woman would do.

She turned tail and ran.

The wine glass crashed to the floor. The door leading to the back deck banged behind her. Molly tore across the wooden deck and into her yard. Instinctively, she headed for the closest signs of human habitation—the light spilling from her neighbor's back windows.

The oleander hedge proved only a minor obstacle. She crashed through it, not even wincing when the thin, leafy branches whipped at her bare legs and slashed her arms. She was so intent on who was behind her that she didn't see the still figure ahead of her. A moment later, she plowed right into him.

"What the…!"

Sam stumbled back, grabbing at the body plastered against his. Small, high breasts flattened against his chest. A hip bone crunched into his. Instant, electric awareness jolted through him, firing nerves from his knees to his neck.

Even before she'd cannonballed into him, he'd recognized his neighbor. Now, he recognized the fact that she packed more curves on her slender frame than the baggy, gray tunic she'd worn last night had suggested.

Hard on the heels of that stomach-clenching discovery came the realization that she'd added wine to her regular beer consumption. From the light, fruity fumes rising in waves to assault his senses, she'd already downed several glasses too many.

Only after he'd untangled his arms and legs from
hers and stepped back a pace did Sam realize that
she hadn't downed all her wine. If the wet splotch
that had transferred from her chest to his shirt was
any indication, she was wearing a good portion of
the bottle...and little else, he noted with a sudden
tightening of his throat.

"Someone's in my house!"

The panic in her voice snapped Sam's attention
from her bare belly button. "What?"

"Someone's in my house," she repeated, digging
her fingers into his arms. "I heard him moving."

The possibility flashed into Sam's mind that his
tipsy neighbor got her kicks by reporting imaginary
assaults and attacks. As quickly as the thought came,
he dismissed it. He could see she wasn't drunk, despite the wine she was wearing, and he'd been
around enough to recognize real fear when he saw
it.

He'd flown F-15s in Desert Storm. Later, he'd
commanded a detachment of test pilots. The men and
women he served with knew how to mask their inner
doubts and fears, but Sam had enough experience
under his belt to recognize the tight lines at the corners of the eyes. The quick glance at the distant sky
when no one was looking. The grin and the cocky
thumbs-up that was as much a prayer as a promise.
The swagger that disguised all doubts, all private
fears.

Molly Duncan didn't try to disguise anything. Her
frightened green eyes grabbed at his gut. Her full

mouth trembled. Her fingers dug into Sam's forearms like talons. Something or someone had shaken her right down to her pink-painted toenails.

Through the silvery hedge, Sam gave her stucco house a quick, searching once-over. He didn't see anything or anyone moving in the brightly lit kitchen. Darkness shadowed the rest of the house.

"There's someone there," she insisted, twisting around to follow his narrowed gaze. "Or there was."

"Did you see him?"

"No. I was in the kitchen and I heard a thump and I ran."

"A thump? What kind of a thump?"

A flicker of impatience pushed some of the fright from her eyes. "How do I know what kind? A thump is a thump."

She was recovering, Sam thought. Fast.

"Then I heard a squeak," she added in a rush. "Like sneakers walking on the tile."

"Go inside and call 911."

He disengaged her clawlike grip and started for the hedge. With a small shriek, she grabbed his arm again.

"You can't go over there. Not alone. Wait for the police!"

"I'm just going to watch the exits, in case whoever or whatever you heard decides to depart the premises before the police arrive. Go on, make the call."

"But...."

"Lock the patio door behind you."

Sam went in low and slow and very, very quiet. He'd grown up hunting with his father and brothers on their northern Arizona spread. Air Force jungle and desert survival schools had refined those silent, predatory skills to the point that Sam had no doubt of his ability to observe without being observed.

It didn't take him long to made a quick circuit of Molly's house. The back door still yawned open from her hasty exit. The garage and front doors remained shut. Sam didn't see any signs of forced entry, but he did find a first-floor window that gave when he tested it. Frowning, he returned to the front of the house just as a squad car pulled up in his driveway.

Molly rushed out of Sam's front door to greet the officer. A backup car arrived in the drive at the same time Sam did. The patrolmen took a disjointed report from Molly and a considerably more coherent one from Sam.

"I didn't leave that window unlocked," she protested. "I'm sure I didn't."

"We'll check it out, ma'am. You'd better wait in the Major's house until we go through yours. You, too, sir."

A still nervous Molly retreated back inside the house. She stationed herself in the tiled foyer, bending a bit to stare through the narrow windows beside the front door. Sam tried *not* to stare at her purple satin boxer shorts. He really tried. The effort raised a small sweat on his temples.

His neighbor wasn't feeling the same heat, though.

She curled one bare foot over the other and wrapped her arms around her waist, as if to ward off a chill. Belatedly, Sam realized that she was under the arctic blasts coming from the air-conditioning vents. He'd gotten in the habit of keeping the house cool during his workouts.

Tearing his appreciative gaze from those clinging purple shorts, he headed down the hall to turn up the thermostat. A quick detour to the laundry room retrieved a well-washed yellow T-shirt showing one of the 442d Test Squadron's F-15s in flight over the desert.

"Here. You'd better put this on before you catch cold."

She spun around, startled by his gruff offer. When he saw her face in full light for the first time, Sam was more than a little startled himself. It took him a moment to identify the brown, peeling stripe laid across her nose and cheeks as some kind of a facial mask. He was still staring at the crusted layer when she reached for the T-shirt.

"Thanks." Her smile tried for grateful and came up shaky. "This wet top and the idea of someone prowling through my house is enough to raise goose bumps all over my skin."

That wet top was enough to raise a few goose bumps on Sam's skin, too. More than a few.

"I wouldn't want you to catch cold and sue me."

He'd meant the oblique reference to the scorching letter she'd sent his contractor, threatening legal action if he touched so much as a leaf of her oleanders, as a joke, as nothing more than an attempt to ease the tension that radiated from her in waves. She didn't take it as one.

"No, I'm sure you wouldn't," she zinged back, tugging the oversized shirt on over her head.

Sam waited until she'd settled the yellow cotton shirt over her hips. "I was kidding, you know."

"I wasn't," she replied coolly. "In my letter, I mean."

"A few scrawny bushes aren't worth going to court over. We'll work something out."

Her mouth settled into a pucker. "I spent most of my landscaping budget on those scrawny bushes. They're not coming down without a fight."

How the hell could the woman manage both scared and stubborn at the same time? Not to mention sexy as hell? A tiny tendril of pain started to curl around the base of Sam's skull.

"We'll work something out," he repeated firmly.

With a tight little nod, she turned her attention back to the windows. Sam tried to turn his attention from the long stretch of bare thigh below the hem of his yellow T-shirt. Despite his best efforts, his stomach tightened. At the same moment, the pain at the base of his skull sent out fresh shoots.

Dammit! Ever since he'd butted headfirst through that malfunctioning canopy, he'd lived with this pain. At best, it was a teeth-grinding annoyance. At worst, it felt like the entire Brazilian soccer team was taking free shots at the back of his skull.

The team had been on break until this moment. He

hoped he'd make it through the rest of the night without having to pummel his body and his mind into numbed submission. Now...

Now his neighbor had barreled into his arms and set off all kinds of alarms in his head. Sam knew he should heed the warning signals. Even without the blossoming pain, his instincts told him to back off. The wisest course of action would be to let this aggravating, enticing female sort out her own problems...which is exactly what he might have done if the police hadn't come down Molly's front walk at that moment.

She threw open his door and hurried outside to meet them. Sam followed, a frown settling between his brows as they gave their report.

"We searched the house, ma'am. We didn't find anyone inside."

"Someone was there," she insisted.

"If he was, he's gone now. We need you to take a look through the house and see if anything's missing."

While the backup officer reclaimed his squad car and drove off, Molly led the way into her house. For the second time in as many nights, Sam found himself in her very spacious, very empty living room. He waited with the patrolman while she made a quick inventory of her possessions.

It didn't take long.

"I don't see anything missing," she said slowly.

The officer hitched up his belt. "Well, there's always the possibility that something or someone other than an intruder caused the noise you heard. The house settling, maybe. A rock thrown against the wall by a passing car. I drove over some lava rock in the road in front of your house.''

Nobly, Sam refrained from pointing out that a fresh scattering of rock ended up in the road every time his neighbor tore down her drive.

''What about the shadow I saw on the wall?'' she demanded. ''And the squeaking sound?''

''Lights from a passing car could have caused the shadow, too. I'm not saying that's what it was, you understand, but....''

''Ms. Duncan made another 911 call last night,'' Sam interjected.

''Yeah?''

His interest piqued, the police officer swung back to Molly. She stared at Sam, then the portion of her face not covered in brown went white.

''I heard a man shot. Or...or thought I did.''

Briefly, she ran through last night's bizarre events. The officer made another annotation, then flipped his notebook closed once more.

''There's probably no connection between what you heard last night and tonight, but I'll let Rodriguez and the folks in Investigations know about your suspicion that someone entered your house....''

''Someone did.''

''Yes, well, either Rodriguez or one of the detectives will get back to you. In the meantime, you might want to keep your windows and doors locked and think about a security system.''

"I will."

The waver in her reply had Sam cursing under his breath. He hadn't intended to scare her by bringing up last night's incident. At this point, he didn't know if there was any link between the shooting she'd heard and her unknown intruder tonight. Hell, he didn't even know if she'd really *heard* a shooting. He just thought they should consider all possibilities.

When Molly turned to him, her face pale under its crusty stripe, he saw that she'd considered the possibilities, too, and didn't much like them. Her gaze darted nervously around the room before centering on Sam.

"Would you like a cup of coffee? Or some wine? I opened a bottle just before...." She managed a wobbly smile. "Just before I came charging through the oleanders."

Sam knew he should leave. The pain at the back of his skull hadn't reached the jaw-breaker stage yet. With luck and a few hours of hard, mind-numbing exercise, he could head it off at the pass. More to the point, he knew he should put some distance between himself and his neighbor. Even in his oversized T-shirt and cracked facial mask, she did serious damage to his self-control.

"Coffee would be good," he heard himself reply.

Chapter 3

Since the basic amenities inside Molly's home didn't run to more than the one easy chair, scattered pillows and a single stool pulled up to the cobalt blue kitchen counter, she and Sam took their coffee to the back deck. There the builder had incorporated two long, curved-backed benches into the railing that defined the rectangular deck.

Molly flipped on the spots and settled on one bench, tucking a bare foot under her. Her neighbor's oversized yellow T-shirt settled around her like a cloud, covering her from neck to knee.

Sam rested his hips against the rail beside her. In the bright wash of light coming from the spots mounted high on the wall, he looked solid and reassuring. He'd *felt* solid and reassuring, too, she remembered, when she'd flung herself into his arms and wrapped herself around him like a wet sponge.

Thinking about how she'd gone chest-to-chest with the Major, Molly squirmed on the cushionless bench. As Henderson had reminded her only a little while ago, they had yet to resolve their property differences. She'd surprised herself by offering him coffee. He'd surprised her even more by accepting it. She wasn't exactly sure why she'd extended that rash invitation, except that her empty, echoing house didn't seem quite as...welcoming...at this moment as it usually did.

"I'm sorry I barreled into you earlier," she said, breaking the stillness of the star-studded night.

"No problem." His mouth curved in a half smile. "I survived four older brothers and almost fifteen years in the military. I've taken worse hits over the years."

She could believe it. Sam Henderson didn't look like the kind of man who went out of his way to avoid trouble, with his brothers or anyone else. Under the bright patio lights, she couldn't miss the blunt angle to his chin or the slight flattening at the bridge of his nose.

Even his clothes seemed to reflect his rugged individualism. He wore his jeans like someone who felt completely at home in them. His soft blue cotton shirt sported a little designer logo on the pocket, but he'd rolled the sleeves up to reveal strong, tanned forearms. Tonight, his dark brown hair had been tamed with a neat side part, unlike last night when

the short layers had sheened with sweat and stood up
in spikes.

Thinking about last night, and tonight, and the
possibility of a connection between the two, Molly
suddenly shivered. The abrupt movement slopped
coffee over the mug and into her lap.

"Oh, no!"

Just in time, she yanked up the T-shirt hem and
thrust her legs to one side. The hot liquid missed her
skin, but spread a soppy brown stain across the cotton. She stared at the splotch in dismay. First the
wine. Now coffee. What else could she spill all over
herself tonight? What else could happen tonight?

"I'm sorry," she said again. "I'll get the stain out,
I promise."

To her horror, her voice wobbled. Even worse, the
hand holding her half-full mug still shook.

Sam reached down and relieved her of the mug.
"Don't worry about it."

But she did. For some reason, the stain spreading
across the shirtfront assumed the proportions of a
near tragedy. Helplessly, Molly grabbed the shirt
hem and twisted it into a tight screw, over and over,
as if she could wring out both the coffee and the fear
that had suddenly invaded her life.

Sam's brows pushed down as he watched his
neighbor's jerky movements. He understood her sudden attack of nerves. He'd seen these kinds of delayed reactions often enough after a dangerous mis-
sion. Concern slid into sympathy, then into a need to
soothe her.

Careful, he told himself. Go real, real careful here. He didn't need to get tangled up with a woman wearing a pungent combination of beer, wine and chocolate hazelnut decaf, for God's sake, any more than he needed the pain streaking up the back of his skull. The way her full mouth trembled shouldn't hit him in the gut. The sheen of tears she furiously blinked back shouldn't curl his hands into fists, either.

Oh, hell. He couldn't take seeing her twist the shirt into knots like that, any more than he could take her sniffles. Hunkering down, he laid his hands over hers. She lifted her face with its cracked and peeling mask to his, and Sam knew he was in trouble.

Big trouble.

"It's okay," he said, gentling his voice. "It's okay, Molly."

She scowled, then glanced down at their joined hands. A small piece of brownish crust flaked off her left cheek and landed on Sam's bent knee, which caused her to scowl even more.

His heart twisted. Resigning himself to the inevitable, he nudged her to one side of the bench and eased in beside her. His arm went around her shoulders, drawing her into his side.

"It's okay, sweetheart."

The endearment didn't mean anything. Sam knew it. Molly obviously knew it, too. She resisted a bit, keeping herself stiff in his loose hold.

"I can't believe I'm acting like such a twit," she muttered. "I don't usually come apart at the seams like this."

"You're not coming apart. You've had a traumatic night. Two traumatic nights. You're just experiencing a delayed reaction. Relax, Molly."

She sank slowly against his chest. To Sam's consternation, she felt as though she'd been carved specifically to fit him. He kept his arms loose and his hands above the swell of her hips, but he experienced a delayed reaction of his own when she shifted to find a more comfortable position.

Gritting his teeth, he willed himself to stay loose. The determined effort sent pain shooting up the side of his skull. For a moment the stars splashed across the sky overhead blurred.

"...you do so late at night, Sam?"

Slowly, the stars regained their luster. The pain became bearable. He picked up the question in Molly's voice, if not her actual words.

"What?"

"What do you do so late at night?"

"I work out. Sometimes I putter in the garage."

"I've seen you out there early in the mornings, when I leave for work. Do you stay up all night?"

"Sometimes."

"Why? Are you part vampire or allergic to sleep or something?"

"I don't need much sleep."

She wasn't letting him get away with that. Tilting her head back, she frowned up at him. "Why not?"

Sam wasn't ready to tell her about the pain. He hadn't told anyone, not even his brothers, how bad it got at times. He'd been sure he would conquer it in time. Now, he wasn't so sure. Nor were the docs.

Instead, he answered the question in her eyes with a small, careless shrug. "I guess I got used to irregular hours in the Air Force."

She was quiet for a while. Sam could feel the tension in her limbs slowly easing. Contrarily, the more she relaxed against him, the more he had to fight the urge to tighten his arms around her.

"What did you do?" she murmured. "When you were in the Air Force?"

"I flew test aircraft," he replied with considerable understatement.

Flying didn't begin to describe what he'd done as a test pilot. Sometimes, he'd throttled to full power and flung his experimental aircraft right at the sun. Sometimes, he'd hurtled it straight down. He'd stressed the wings, stressed the weapons load, stressed himself with every twisting spiral.

"And now you're retired?"

"Yes."

Sam still had trouble with the word. Retired. At thirty-six. The Medical Evaluation Board had assured him that they'd consider removing him from the Temporary Disability Retired List when and if he conquered the headaches. The possibility seemed as remote tonight as it had six months ago.

"Were you stationed at Nellis?" she asked, her voice drowsy and indistinct.

"Yes, I was."

He rested his chin on the top of her head. Her mix

of scents tugged at his senses. Shampoos, coffee, that crazy, crackly stuff she wore on her face. The feel of her body slanted against his tugged at more than his senses.

"I was assigned to the Four-forty-second Test and Evaluation Squadron," he told her, as much to distract himself as to keep the conversational ball rolling. "We conducted operational tests for Air Combat Command on new hardware and equipment upgrades in simulated combat environments."

"Mmm?"

The mumble could have signaled interest or incipient unconsciousness. Sam suspected it was the latter. He hesitated, debating whether to continue.

He hadn't talked about the life that had ended the night he went headfirst through that damned canopy in a long time. Too long. Somehow, it was easier here with Molly. The calm night air and black velvet sky seemed to wrap them in a private world. More to the point, the casual, one-sided conversation seemed just what she needed after her earlier fright.

"The four-forty-second is a mixed unit," he said slowly. "We flew fighters and attack helicopters. Most of the equipment we tested is classified, but I can tell you that we did a lot of night flying, and that we developed new methods of employing the Low Altitude Navigation and Targeting Infrared for Night system."

He knew his listener was falling asleep even before she gave one of those reflexive little jerks that come with relaxation of the muscles. He smiled at her mumbled apology, and deliberately kept his voice to a low, steady monotone. Not so deliberately, he tightened his hold and brought her onto his lap.

The low bench back cut into his back. The wooden seat numbed his butt. He shifted, angling his body into the wedge formed by the angle of the rails. When Molly shifted as well, draping herself across him from shoulder to hip, the singeing contact instantly upped Sam's discomfort factor by a multiple of ten. Her breath warmed his neck. Her legs tangled with his. Sam refused to let himself dwell on the way her breasts flattened against his chest, or the long length of thigh that stretched beneath the hem of his squadron T-shirt. Despite his best efforts, his lower body went hard.

Great! The pounding at the base of his skull was bad enough. He didn't need this tight, coiling ache in his belly to add to it. Briefly, he debated taking her inside before the still-warm desert night cooled.

From long, painful experience, Sam knew that cooling wouldn't occur until just before dawn. He'd spent enough nights watching the moon sink and listening to the distant coyotes. If he concentrated on something other than the soft tush in his lap and the warm wash of breath against his neck, he could take another hour or two. By then, his prickly neighbor should have regrouped, regained her equilibrium, maybe even revived enough to resume her battle over the blasted bushes.

Sam eyed the tall, silvery bushes. He supposed he'd have to get the contractor to redesign the pool.

Maybe angle it a bit to give him the length he needed for straight laps. His doctor had recommended swimming instead of pumping iron to refocus his mind when the headaches threatened to get out of control.

Like now.

Dammit! This one was going to be a real winner. After six weeks in the hospital and almost as many months in physical therapy, Sam knew the signs. Cursing to himself, he started counting the stars.

Molly woke slowly. Her cheek felt numb where it pressed against something hard and unyielding. Her neck ached from bending at an odd angle. Overriding those minor annoyances, though, was the delicious sensation of curling into warmth and the steady, reassuring drum of a strong heartbeat in her ear.

For a confused moment, she thought she was back in Boston, snuggled up in Brady's arms. Mumbling, she slid a hand across the chest under her cheek. Her hips wiggled a deeper nest in his lap.

Strange. Brady's chest had never felt this hard or this muscled before. Nor, Molly thought with sleepy surprise, had she ever heard him mutter such a colorful curse under his breath.

The realization that the hard, contoured chest under her palm didn't belong to her former fiancé registered on Molly's consciousness at about the same instant she identified the southwestern drawl in that curse.

She pushed upright, dismayed to find Sam's tight-clenched jaw just inches from her own. Oh, great!

Not only had she draped herself across her neighbor like an afghan, she'd dropped off into total oblivion in the midst of his telling her about his Air Force days. Mortified, she tried to scramble off his lap. His arms flexed for a brief instant, holding her in place, then dropped. In an undignified scramble, Molly got to her feet and tugged the yellow T-shirt down over her hips.

"I'm sorry," she mumbled for what seemed like the umpteenth time that night.

Her embarrassment doubled when she saw Sam's face. Distant and withdrawn, it held none of the understanding he'd shown when he'd taken her into his arms...when?...a few minutes ago? An hour ago?

"I didn't mean to fall asleep on you," she said in a strangled voice.

"No problem."

The response came out short and too clipped. He got to his feet, unfolding his body with a stiffness at odds with his earlier easy grace. Once upright, he held himself rigidly erect, as though the mere act of moving was an effort.

Good grief. Had her dead weight stiffened him up like that? How long had she sprawled on top of him and pinned him to that bench, anyway? He answered her silent question before she asked it.

"I was going to wake you up in a few minutes. It can get chilly out here just before dawn."

Dawn! Molly shot a disbelieving look at the eastern horizon. Sure enough, the sky showed a distant tint of golden red.

"I can't believe we spent almost the whole night on that bench."

"Believe it."

Something that might have been a smile started at the corners of his mouth. It twisted suddenly, and ended in a near grimace. "I have to go," he said abruptly. "Why don't we take another walk through the house before I leave? Just so you feel comfortable about going inside."

Molly had to admit that she felt decidedly *un*comfortable at that moment, not to mention embarrassed and confused. Her tumbling emotions had nothing to do with a reluctance to reenter her house. They did, however, have a whole lot to do with Sam Henderson's Jekyll-and-Hyde personality.

"Thanks, but you don't need to go through the house. I've already, uh, imposed on you enough."

Imposed hardly came close to describing the way she'd pinned the man to the bench, but she hoped her slight understatement might at least crack the rigid cast to his face. No such luck.

"I'll do a quick sweep," he bit out.

He disappeared into the house, leaving Molly now almost as irritated as she was confused. What was with this guy, anyway? Had she dreamed his friendliness earlier? Had he really drawn her onto his lap and cradled her? Maybe she'd just sort of landed there, and he'd been too polite to shove her away.

No, she decided, polite didn't figure among Sam Henderson's more significant character traits...as he demonstrated when he returned a few moments later.

"All clear. Good night."

Her jaw sagging, Molly stared at his back as he marched stiff-legged across her yard. A moment later, the oleanders swallowed him up.

She snapped her mouth shut. She had no idea what the heck Sam's problem was, but she darned well wasn't going to spend the little that was left of the night trying to figure it out. With luck, she could grab two or three more hours of sleep before she had to get ready for work. Spinning around, Molly marched inside the house. The patio door banged shut behind her.

In a distant corner of his brain, Sam recorded the snapping sound, just as he'd recorded the surprise on Molly's face when he'd left her so abruptly. He couldn't think about either at this moment, though. He needed all his concentration just to put one foot in front of the other and make it to his own back door.

He couldn't believe he'd been such a fool! He'd known better than to just sit there, breathing in his neighbor's unique, intriguing combination of scents, while the demons in his head took possession of his body. He should have put her out of his arms hours ago. Gone back to his own house. Pounded the damned pain into submission with a grinding workout.

He knew his abrupt departure had bewildered her. Better bewilderment than pity, Sam thought savagely. He didn't need her pity. Any more than he needed commiserating slaps on the back from his former squadron mates or worried calls from his brothers. He'd beat this thing. He'd prove the doctors wrong and beat it, and he'd do it without doping himself up with painkillers every night.

Until he did, though, he sure as hell wasn't much use to anyone...particularly a green-eyed, long-legged blonde who seemed to attract trouble like a magnet. Slamming his own patio door shut with a force that added another bright color to the kaleido-scope whirling through his head, Sam stripped off his shirt. His mouth grim, he headed for the well-worn leather bench.

Molly puzzled over her neighbor's strange behav-ior off and on for most of the next morning...until the call from the Las Vegas Police Department drove all other thoughts right out of her head.

It came just after lunch, as she was walking out of her office for a meeting with the director of the new fifty-four-million-dollar Star Trek museum and entertainment center at the Las Vegas Hilton. The spectacular fifty-four-million-dollar center had just opened, and the director had promised Molly and a number of the media a sneak preview. A long time trekkie, she was looking forward to the tour. Impa-tiently, she leaned back over her desk to catch the phone.

"Molly Duncan."

"Hello, Ms. Duncan. This is Detective Kaplan, from the LVPD Homicide Unit. I wanted to let you know that we traced the call you made at one-twelve yesterday morning.''

Her heart skipped a beat. ''Yes?''

''The number you dialed belongs to a man named Joe Bennett. His rap sheet lists a number of aliases, but we know him as Joey the Horse.''

''Rap sheet? You mean he's a criminal?''

''A small-time drug dealer with a weakness for the ponies. He also supplements his income by pimping for the high rollers. Or he did. He won't be supplementing anything anymore.''

''Is he...?'' Molly gripped the phone. ''Is he dead?''

''As the proverbial doornail,'' Kaplan confirmed with a notable lack of sympathy for the deceased. ''The landlord let our guys into his apartment this afternoon. They found Joey with a nice, neat hole in the middle of his forehead and a not so neat one in his chest.''

Molly sagged against the edge of her desk. Over and over, a desperate plea echoed in her mind.

''Oh, God.''

''I'm in court this afternoon on another case,'' the detective continued, ''but I'd like to talk to you about your phone call. Can you swing by the station in the morning? Hello? Ms. Duncan?''

''What?'' She shook herself out of the shocked trance. ''Oh. Yes, of course.''

''Ten o'clock okay?''

''Ten o'clock,'' she repeated numbly, then Kaplan shifted gears with a disconcerting suddenness.

"I understand you also reported hearing some noises in your house last night?"

"Yes, I did."

"There's probably no connection between the two incidents, but until we clear up this business with Joey, I've asked the city desk to increase the patrols through your neighborhood. Call 911 if you see or hear anything that makes you nervous."

Anything that made her *more* nervous, Molly corrected silently as she dropped the receiver onto the cradle. She stared at the phone as if it were an instrument of evil.

She'd heard someone shoot another human being. Really and truly shoot him. The reality stunned her. And curled her stomach into a tight, frightened knot. She was still standing motionless beside her desk when her boss whirled in on a cloud of Arpege and brisk efficiency.

"Hey, girl! I thought you had a two o'clock at the Hilton."

"I did. Uh, I do."

The mumbled reply brought Davinia's perfectly arched brows snapping together. "What's the matter? You look like you've seen a ghost."

"I think the operative word is heard, not seen," Molly said weakly.

"Huh?"

"The police just called."

"Really?" Davinia hitched a hip on the corner of Molly's desk and swung a long, nyloned leg. "Did they trace the call you made?"

Molly nodded. "Evidently I called a Mr. Joey the Horse Bennett, a drug dealer and occasional pimp."

"You're kidding!"

"I wish!"

Gathering her scattered thoughts, she relayed her brief conversation with Detective Kaplan. When she finished, her boss swung her leg in a slow, thoughtful arc. Her three-inch clear acrylic heel caught the light and threw back a rainbow of color.

"A drug-dealing pimp with a New Jersey accent, a weakness for the horses and a hole in his forehead. This doesn't sound good, girl. Not good at all."

"As a matter of fact, it sounded awful," Molly replied with a little shudder. "You should have heard him, pleading with the killer for his life."

"Well, yes, but that wasn't what I meant."

Waving a hand tipped with long, silvered nails, Davinia dismissed the now-deceased drug dealer with the same casual callousness Detective Kaplan had.

"Las Vegas has pretty well cleaned up its act in the past decade or so," she said, "but there are still a few of the old school around. Men with connections."

"Connections?"

"You know, the old families."

Molly stared at her boss in dismay. "Are you suggesting that I overheard a mob execution?"

"It's a possibility."

Groaning, she reached for her purse. "Thanks a lot! Now I won't get any sleep tonight, either."

Davinia took her lower lip between blindingly

white teeth. "Why don't you come stay with me for a few days? Just until the police work this case?"

Molly almost took her up on the offer. Somehow, the thought of going back to her empty house didn't hold quite the same appeal it had before. Davinia had just moved the latest candidate for husband number four into her condo, however, and Molly didn't want to impede the matrimonial tryouts.

"You don't need any more company," she replied. "You've got Antonio."

"Nonsense. He'll love having two women to practice his techniques on. Not that he needs much practice," she added with a wicked grin.

Since the hunky Latino had recently graduated with top honors from massage school, Molly didn't doubt it. She did, however, doubt that he'd appreciate another woman's presence in the house. Particularly when her boss had hinted that she'd instituted a program of total seduction and surrender...her seduction and Antonio's surrender.

Gracefully, Molly refused Davinia's offer and headed home. It was only as she pulled into her driveway and spotted the lights in Sam's house that she realized a good part of her reason for refusing Davinia's offer was the knowledge that her confusing, intriguing neighbor was only a hedge away.

Chapter 4

Molly leaned down to snag the yellow T-shirt from the dryer. When she pulled it out, a fragrant cloud of fabric softener came with it. Holding the garment up to the light, she examined its front. After two washings, the brown coffee splotch had pretty well disappeared. The little that remained was so faint that it blended right in with the faded, streaky yellow.

Laying the shirt on top of the dryer, she smoothed the wrinkles with her palms. The faded blue patch on the front caught her gaze. The lettering below it read 442d TES, whatever that meant.

Vaguely Molly recalled Sam telling her about the unit he'd been assigned to at Nellis. She'd hovered somewhere between sleepy exhaustion and total unconsciousness at the time, so she had only hazy memories of his voice rumbling under her ear. The sensation of Sam's thighs shifting under hers hadn't exactly added to her powers of concentration, either. Nor had the steely strength of his arms folded around her.

Thinking back to those hours on the deck, Molly had to admit that Sam's solid strength had given her the oddest sense of comfort. Not that she really needed it, of course. She didn't want any man flexing his muscles in her life, even figuratively. She'd had enough of that with Brady. Still, for a few hours, she felt warm and comfortable and safe in Sam's arms.

She frowned, disturbed by the idea that she required anything or anyone to feel safe in her own home. This was her castle. Her sanctuary.

She glanced through the laundry room door at the brightly lit kitchen. On any other night, the sand-colored plaster walls with their border of blue and gold Aztec sun signs would give her a small thrill of pride, just as the long, clean sweep of cobalt blue counter fed her need for color and brightness.

Tonight she saw only the kitchen's empty corners. Slowly, she shifted her gaze to the windows. A silvery path of light spilled from her neighbor's high living room windows and traced across her yard. Molly contemplated the shimmering trail for several moments. Although she couldn't hear Sam's music, thank goodness, that trail of light lured her like a beacon.

Folding the T-shirt, she decided to follow that beacon. After a quick detour to the powder room just off the kitchen to twist her hair up in a clear plastic clip decorated with pink rhinestone flamingos, courtesy of the famous hotel's gift shop, she slipped into a pair of similarly decorated plastic mules. She smiled, thinking how the gaudy accessories that were so much a part of the Vegas scene would have brought a pained look to her former fiancé's face. Molly, on the other hand, loved them. Thank goodness she'd walked away from Brady before the man had smothered her or she'd strangled him.

On that cheerful thought, she marched out the kitchen door and followed the silvery path through her backyard to Sam's. She wouldn't linger at his place. Not after his abrupt good-bye and hasty retreat this morning. She'd just return his T-shirt and give him an update on Detective Kaplan's call, keeping a nice, neighborly distance in the process.

Molly had pushed through the hedge before she realized that she should have approached his house from the front and rung the doorbell. It was a little tacky to stroll into his backyard and walk right up to his patio. It was even more tacky to gape at the sight that greeted her through the open windows.

Sam lay astride a narrow leather bench, wearing only a pair of blue nylon athletic shorts and a grimace. Above him towered the jungle of gleaming steel bars Molly had rushed past to get to a phone last night. She didn't rush anywhere tonight. Tonight, she stood rooted to the patio, her feet planted as firmly as her oleanders, and watched her neighbor in motion.

He moved to a rhythm that appeared as strenuous

as it was beautiful. On a beat that only he could hear, his tendons corded. His glistening muscles gathered. A black column of weights lifted almost to the top of the steel structure. A moment later, he sucked in a breath and relaxed. The weights plunged.

Slowly, he gathered himself and flexed once more.

Molly stood in the shadows, transfixed. She wasn't into sweat herself. In fact, she generally tried to avoid any activity that raised even the faintest hint of moisture on her skin...with one or two notable exceptions, of course. She had to admit, though, that the sheer perfection of Sam's movements gave a new perspective to the whole question of exercise.

Molly hated to interrupt him, but she wasn't into voyeurism any more than sweat. Not usually, anyway. After watching Sam in motion, she could almost understand how masses of people got off on purely spectator sports. Clutching the folded T-shirt to her chest, she rapped on the glass patio door. He didn't hear her. She tried again, knuckling the glass with a little more force. Still no response. Finally, she gave the tempered sliding door a solid whack.

The weights froze, and Sam twisted on the bench. He pinned her with a narrow, piercing glance, his face wearing the same expression it had this morning. Hard. Tight. Unwelcoming.

Wishing now that she'd stuffed the T-shirt and a note in his mailbox, Molly pasted on a smile that strove for a balance between neighborly and distant. She didn't want the man to think that she'd come running to him in a fright again or that she was hounding him. Considering their brief and somewhat brittle acquaintance, though, she supposed he couldn't think anything else.

Thankfully, his grim expression eased when he took in her unfrantic face. Peeling himself off the bench, he reached for the gray sweatshirt draped over one of the crossbars. By the time he unlocked the patio doors and slid them open, he looked almost friendly. Only a woman who'd spent the night in his arms might notice that the creases at either side of his mouth went far too deep to constitute a smile.

"Hello, neighbor. Everything all right on the far side of the oleanders?"

"More or less."

He cocked his head. His dark brown hair glistened, shining almost black in the overhead light.

"Is my music bothering you again? Sorry. I thought I had the volume turned down low enough to keep it from carrying."

Molly hadn't even noticed the lament for a lost dog...or was it for an ex-wife?...threading through the air until Sam mentioned it.

"No, the volume's fine."

He invited her inside, and she declined with a little shake of her head.

"I just wanted to return your T-shirt. I got most of the coffee stain out."

"You shouldn't have bothered. The thing's seen better days. Much better days," he added, taking it from her outstretched hands. His eyes went to the patch on the front. He thumbed the lettering for a moment, then shook his head, as if to clear it of unwanted memories, and tossed the shirt aside.

"Sure you won't come in? I don't have any hazelnut decaf, but I think I can scare up some instant. Or some cold beer, if you prefer."

Molly decided it was time to correct that particular misconception. "I don't drink the stuff," she informed him loftily. "I just wear it."

His mouth kicked up to a half smile. "I hadn't noticed."

"Liar. I probably flaked all over your shirt last night."

"What are a few flakes between neighbors? Look, why don't you come in? I'll turn off the CD player, I promise. You won't have to suffer through Buck and company, if that's what's holding you back."

Molly knew darn well what was holding her back... Sam Henderson's on-again, off-again charm. In the early hours just before dawn, his icy stare had frozen her to her deck. Now, that half grin of his was causing a minor meltdown in her circulatory system. Much against her better judgment, she caved.

"Well, if you promise...."

He slid the patio door shut behind her and crossed to the washed-oak cabinets built into the wall beside the fireplace. The high-tech electronic equipment that filled the cabinets looked powerful and sophisticated enough to launch the space shuttle *Atlantis*. They'd certainly sent Bucky Boy soaring through the night on a number of previous occasions.

Sam punched a few buttons, and the low, lonesome wail segued into the haunting strains of a violin concerto. Molly blinked in surprise. Buck Randall and Mozart? On the same CD player? Her conflicting impressions of her neighbor took a turn into serious confusion.

"Come on into the kitchen while I zap some water," he invited.

She trailed him through the house, seeing it with an eye for the details she hadn't noticed last night. Aside from the soaring, two-storied great room which Sam had turned into his own personal gym, the rest of the place held a mix of comfortable, masculine furnishings and artwork from every corner of the world. Asian batiks and carved African masks hung in a dazzling display on one wall. A collection of delicate watercolors depicting European street scenes decorated the long central hall.

But it was the well-furnished and fully equipped kitchen that gave Molly a real pang. She sighed, lusting instantly for the rectangular, washed-oak table and six high-backed chairs. Behind the table, a glass-and-brass étagère drew her envious eye. The piece took up most of the far wall, and displayed to perfection a truly remarkable collection of beer steins.

While Sam rummaged in the cupboard for cups, Molly examined the collection. Colorful coats of arms decorated the front of each stein, and military figures exquisitely detailed in pewter and silver perched atop the lids. Some of the figures sat astride prancing steeds. Others stood at attention or lunged with weapons drawn. All wore tall shakos and what looked like fur cloaks thrown over one shoulder. Enchanted, Molly traced a finger along a raised silver sword.

"These are beautiful."

"They're Prussian regimentals. I picked them up when I was stationed in Germany a few years ago. They have pictures glazed into the bottom that become visible when the owner drains his beer."

"Really?" Molly thumbed back a lid.

"Most of the scenes depict the unit's arms or insignia. A few are more, uh, artistic."

"So I see," she drawled.

Letting the pewter lid drop on the over-endowed and underdressed fräulein who smirked up at her, she settled into one of the chairs. Another twinge of envy attacked her as she glanced around the comfortable kitchen.

Aside from the living room/gym, Sam had managed to make his house into a home in a remarkably short period of time. Or, she wondered suddenly, did he owe the comfortable arrangements to the sultry-voiced female who'd answered the phone the first time Molly had called to complain about his music?

Or had she even called Sam that first time? Maybe she'd misdialed then, too. The thought sent a shiver down Molly's spine and reminded her all too graphically of her second reason for pushing through the oleanders.

"The police contacted me today," she told her host. "They traced the number I dialed the other night."

He shot her a quick look over the steaming mugs of hot water. "And?"

"And it belongs to a man named Joey the Horse Bennett...recently deceased."

Sam swore. Quietly. Succinctly. Dumping spoonfuls of dark granules into each mug, he gave them a quick stir and joined Molly at the table.

"Tell me the details."

She took a sip of coffee first, finding that the telling seemed to get harder, not easier. With each repetition, the victim became more that just a disembodied voice. She imagined a short, wiry dark-haired man. Heard his desperate pleas. Tried not to see a bullet hole blossom in his forehead.

"A Detective Kaplan in Homicide asked me to come downtown tomorrow at ten," she finished, swirling the dark liquid in her mug. "He wants to go over exactly what I heard."

"You okay with that?"

She looked up to find Sam studying her with a frown in his gray eyes.

"No," she admitted. "I get a little queasy every time I think about that phone call. My phantom visitor last night didn't exactly help matters, either."

"I did a walk-around of your house before you got home tonight," Sam said, surprising her. "All the doors and windows were secure. I'll make another check after you go back inside."

Molly didn't think he'd intended that as a hint for her to leave, but she decided to use it as an exit cue. Pushing her mug aside, she rose.

"Thanks. I'm enough of a coward to appreciate the offer."

"No need to rush off. You haven't finished your coffee."

She didn't tell him that she'd lingered too long as it was. For a belligerent ex-military type with vampire habits and a Jekyll-and-Hyde personality, Sam Henderson could certainly turn on the charm when he wanted to. She'd better get the heck out of Dodge, or in this case, out of his beautiful kitchen, before she did something stupid. Such as get too friendly with a man who turned his emotions on and off like a faucet.

"Coffee's the last thing I really need tonight," she confessed, detouring around the steel jungle of his living room. "My boss suggested that I overheard a mob execution. That cheerful thought is enough to keep me awake without the added stimulus of caffeine."

"A mob execution," Sam echoed, frowning. "I suppose that's one possibility. This Joey character could have welched on his bets or gotten crosswise of a major drug distributor."

"Hey! For a guy who's trying to reassure me by checking my doors and windows, you're going about it all wrong! Besides, the man I heard shoot Joey the Horse didn't sound like a mobster."

"Oh? Have you carried on conversations with a lot of mafioso before?"

She threw him a nasty look. "This guy came across as educated, sophisticated."

"You think today's hoods aren't?"

"Okay, okay. What if it was the mob who rubbed him out? Unless the police can put a face to the voice I heard, it won't make any difference."

She didn't know who she was trying to convince, herself or Sam. In any case, she got the answer to her question the very next morning.

Molly had only visited City Hall once before. Her boss had taken her down to meet the mayor and city council, who maintained a close working relationship with the Convention Center. At the time, the multistory elliptical glass structure on the corner of Fourth and Stewart hadn't particularly impressed Molly. Nor had the shallow, empty fountain in front of the building. Devoid of even a trickle of water, the dry fountain had struck her as incongruous in a city bursting with vibrant energy.

The interval between Molly's first and second trip to the municipal building hadn't improved its appeal. The grim purpose behind her visit only emphasized its stark, uninviting facade. After asking directions from the receptionist at the front desk, she made her way to the police department located in the rear annex and asked directions to Detective Kaplan's office. A uniformed officer directed her up two flights of stairs and down a long hall.

She found the Homicide Division…and Sam Henderson ensconced in one of the uncomfortable-looking plastic chairs placed in front of a modular desk unit.

He rose at her approach, tall and calm and smiling a little at her surprise. For the first time in their brief acquaintance, he wore something other than jeans, sweats or thigh-skimming athletic shorts. Even in loafers, black slacks and crisp, blue cotton shirt, however, he looked like a man who knew his way around a gym.

Chiding herself for the strange little rush of pleasure his presence generated, Molly inquired what he was doing there.

"Kaplan called this morning and asked me to come in as well. I guess he was hoping that I could add some detail to your initial report. So far, I've come up blank. Here, have a seat."

She had just taken the other chair when a short, compact individual in wrinkled gray slacks and a tan sport coat approached.

"Miss Duncan?" He tossed a file on the desk and held out his hand. "I'm Al Kaplan. Thanks for coming down."

Molly's ear picked up a hint of an accent. German, she was sure. Judging by his dark jowls and sturdy build, the detective had no doubt descended from first-generation immigrants.

"Have you met Major Henderson?" Kaplan shook his head at his own question. "Oh, sure you have. He's your neighbor, the one you lodged the complaint against the night you heard the murder."

Avoiding Sam's sardonic gaze, Molly nodded. "Yes, he is."

"I've read the police reports filed as a result of

your two calls to 911," the detective continued, seating himself opposite the two, "but I'd like go over them with you in detail."

"Both of them?" she asked with a little frown.

"Both of them."

"Why? Do you think there's a chance that the two incidents are related?"

"We can't discount the possibility. You said in your statement that the killer picked up the phone while you were still on the line."

"Yes, he did."

Even now, in the bright light of day, she could hear the echo of the victim's desperate pleading and the killer's cold, calm response.

"You probably shook him as much as he scared you," the detective theorized, shuffling through the files on his desk. "Could be, he decided to check you out. Wouldn't have been hard to track you down. Especially with your name and phone number on Joey's caller ID."

Molly felt the blood drain from her face. "He had caller ID?"

"Yeah. Everyone and his brother's got one of those gadgets these days."

She barely heard the offhand remark. The abstract possibility that the shooting she'd heard was somehow connected to her uninvited guest had been disturbing enough. The fact that the killer had instant access to her name and telephone number at the time of the murder lifted the matter out of the realm of possibility and put it down on just the other side of scary.

"...again exactly what you heard."

She stared at Kaplan, too shaken to reply.

"Ms. Duncan?"

In the seat next to her, Sam cursed under his breath. He hadn't missed the shock that darkened her green eyes or the pallor of her face. He reached for her hand, cradling it between both of his.

"Molly?"

Turning a white, frightened face to his, she gripped his fingers with bruising force. Protective instincts he had no business feeling for this woman leaped into his chest. The need to take her in his arms slammed into him. He restrained himself, but only because Molly released her death grip on his hand at that moment and turned her attention back to Kaplan.

"I'm sorry. The idea that the man I heard fire those shots knew exactly who he was speaking to when he picked up the phone got to me."

The detective picked up a pencil and leaned forward. "Let's talk about that. What, exactly, did he say to you?"

"'Hello.'"

Both Sam and Kaplan waited expectantly. When she didn't volunteer anything more, disappointment flattened the detective's face.

"That's it?" At Molly's nod, he tossed his pencil on top of the reports and scraped a hand across his cheeks. "'Hello' is not going to get us far."

She pulled in a breath. "No, it won't. But I also

heard him talking to Joey before he shot him. He spoke with an accent, faint but definitely upper Midwest. From the way he rounded his vowels, I'd guess Wisconsin or Michigan. He also attended school or worked on the East Coast.''

Kaplan gaped at her. ''You got all that from just a few phrases?''

''Languages are my profession and my specialty,'' she answered with a shrug. ''My grandparents on one side are first-generation Irish, and second-generation Polish on the other. I could swear fluently in Gaelic or in Polish by the time I was three.''

''So how does Gaelic translate to upper Midwestern?''

''My dad worked for the Great Northern Railroad. We moved every few years, and I picked up the local slang wherever we happened to live. Since then, I've studied seven additional languages, including German, French, Japanese and Korean.''

Sam was impressed. Kaplan even more so.

''I'd recognize the man's voice instantly if I heard it again,'' Molly finished.

''*If* you hear it again,'' the detective pointed out. ''I'll run what you gave us through the PD's database to see if we turn up anyone with a Midwestern background and a record. We'll also work the local pawn shops to see if anyone with that particular accent purchased a .38 recently. It's a long shot, but worth a try.''

He flipped the file folder shut, then hesitated. Sam

sensed what was coming next. He felt the worry in his gut even before Kaplan voiced it.

"In the meantime, Ms. Duncan, you'd better stay alert. It also wouldn't hurt to have the locks on your doors changed and a security system installed. Whoever killed Joey the Horse knows who you are and may or may not have paid you a visit already."

"As if I needed that reminder!"

Molly pushed through the outer glass doors into the dry, searing heat. She stood on the broad steps for a moment, face lifted to the sun, willing the warmth to chase away the chill of Kaplan's remark.

Sam saw the pallor under her scattering of freckles and felt the knot cinching his gut tighten another notch. He knew he should walk away. Now, while he still could. He had enough problems of his own without adding Molly Duncan to the list.

But he couldn't just stroll off and leave her to deal with the shock of knowing that a cold-blooded killer had taken her name and phone number off a caller ID unit.

"It may take a while to get that security system installed," he said slowly. "With all the building going on in Vegas these days, I had to wait two weeks for mine."

"Two weeks!"

Dismay darkened her eyes to a deep, shadowed green. Sam held out for five seconds. Ten. Almost a half minute.

"I've got three empty bedrooms at my place," he

forced out. "You're welcome to use one until you get your house wired."

She glanced up, as surprised by the offer as he was by having made it. He saw the polite refusal forming in her eyes and bit back a sigh of relief. He'd offered. He'd done his neighborly duty.

To his consternation, she hesitated. He could almost see her mind working, clicking through her friends and acquaintances. Her brows drew together, carving a little groove down the middle of her forehead.

"Maybe...."

The tentative reply stopped his heart. He held his breath while she nibbled delicately on her lower lip and the heat rose in shimmering waves around them.

"Maybe I'll take you up on that. If you're sure?"

Sam glanced down into her freckle-dusted face. At that moment, he knew he was about to commit what the military termed "a serious mistake in judgment," a catch-all phrase for any irresponsible act leading to total and irrevocable havoc.

"I'm sure."

Chapter 5

"You're staying with the jerk?"

Davinia lifted a perfectly arched brow in disbelief.

"The creep?" she asked melodramatically, as if doubting her subordinate's nod. "The defiler of the airwaves and would-be slayer of oleanders?"

"Only for a night. Two at most."

Or so Molly hoped! Avoiding her boss's incredulous stare, she plopped the thick yellow pages down on her desk. A quick thumbing brought her to the section on burglar alarms.

"I must have missed something here," the older woman mused. "When did your surly neighbor go from obnoxious to so hospitable that you two are going to shack up for the weekend?"

"We're not shacking up," Molly sputtered.

"We're just spending a night or two under the same roof."

"Suuuure you are."

Davinia, as her employee well knew, didn't ascribe to the theory that platonic friendships between men and women were possible, or particularly desirable. Swinging a shapely foot encased in a lizard shoe sporting a three-inch, hourglass shaped heel, she gave her subordinate a speculative once-over.

"Come on, girl. Let's have it. Why are you sleeping with the enemy instead of staying at the condo with Antonio and me this weekend?"

Smiling, Molly ticked off the reasons. "One, because you gave me a fairly detailed outline of what you were going to do to and with Antonio when you got him alone this weekend and I didn't want to get in the way."

"You wouldn't have been in the way...much."

"Two, I need to be at my place to give the security folks access. And, three...?"

"Yes?"

"All right," Molly admitted. "The Major and I have, well, declared a truce."

"Aha!" Her boss's turquoise eyes gleamed. "I knew it."

"A truce, Davinia. That's all." She shoved a hand through her hair. "If I'd been thinking rationally this morning, I would've made arrangements to stay at one of the hotels. I guess that business with the caller ID rattled me."

Her boss's smug expression disappeared. "That

would have shaken me, too.'' She drummed a long nail on the desk. ''Ex-number-three knows some folks in the construction business. Do you want me to see if he can recommend a reliable alarm company?''

''Yes, please!''

By shamelessly exploiting Davinia's ex-husband's connections, Molly arranged for Allied Security Systems to survey her house that very afternoon. She drove home to meet the company rep at four-fifteen.

Surveying the house was one thing, she soon learned. Installing the system was another. After alternately begging, brow-beating, and acting the frightened female...which didn't really take all that much acting...Molly finally wrung a promise from the harassed rep to send a work crew out tomorrow.

''No, wait. Tomorrow's Saturday.'' He shoved his ballcap back and swiped the sweat off his bald crown. ''I've got all three of my crews working overtime on that new housing development off Flamingo Road. Hafta be Sunday. Or Monday, if we run behind.''

''But...''

''That's the best I can do, Ms. Duncan. Take it or leave it.''

Molly blew out a slow breath. ''I'll take it.''

Twilight hung in a soft purple haze outside her bedroom windows when she dumped a sleep shirt and a few vital necessities into a plastic tote decorated with a glittery gold MGM lion.

This house-sharing arrangement with Sam would work, she told herself again. Molly would make it work. She'd get up early and get out of Sam's way. She had plenty to do at the office to keep her busy over the weekend. Allied promised to call when they were ready to come out. She'd meet them here, then move right back into her own home. That way, she'd inconvenience her host and herself as little as possible.

That was the plan, anyway, when Molly slipped on a pair of low-heeled thong sandals in the same cherry red as the short-sleeved top she wore with her jeans, then made her way downstairs.

Sam unfolded himself from the rattan chair in her living room and eyed the little plastic tote. "Do you have everything you need?"

"Everything I need for tonight. Hopefully, I won't have to impose on you longer than that."

"You travel light," he replied with a smile that creased his tanned cheeks. "And as for imposing on me, we've already covered that ground. Several times. I wouldn't have invited you if I didn't want the company."

Given his on-again, off-again personality, Molly wasn't so sure. Tonight, though, she had to admit he was on. Definitely, devastatingly, one-hundred-percent on. His easy smile could charm the bark off a tree. It certainly peeled away a few of Molly's outer layers.

He'd traded the black slacks he'd worn earlier this morning for his customary jeans, but still wore the blue cotton shirt. He'd shoved up the sleeves to his elbows and acquired a small grease stain on one cuff, probably from the Mustang he'd been working on when Molly had pulled into her driveway.

She didn't think he'd been waiting for her specifically since he spent a good number of his evenings bent over the fender of the little red classic, but his solid presence had given her a surprising spurt of pleasure and…okay, she could admit it…relief. When he strolled across their parallel driveways and accompanied her inside her empty house, she'd been more than happy to let him do a quick search of the premises.

As Molly walked beside him now through the deepening twilight, her sandals crunching on the lava rock, she grappled with the disturbing fact that the narrow strip between their properties now seemed more like a safe passage than a hostile fire zone. She didn't like the fact that she'd been frightened out of her own home, but she liked the possibility that a killer might be watching her and her house even less. Sam shouldered open the door to his home, stepping back for her to enter. "Take your pick of the rooms upstairs. Come on down when you're settled and I'll throw some steaks on the grill."

Molly paused with one foot on the stairs. It was well past eight o'clock. She'd made it a point to work late and grab a taco on her way home so she wouldn't impinge on Sam's hospitality any more than she had to. Turning down his offer seemed a bit rude, though.

"I got a fresh shipment of prime cut this morning," he added casually. "Compliments of the Double Bar."

"Okay, I'll bite. What's the Double Bar?"

"A small spread in northern Arizona. The brand is sort of a sideways 'H.'"

"The 'H' standing for Henderson, I assume?"

He nodded, and Molly gave herself a mental pat on the back for correctly placing his faint drawl the first time she'd heard it.

"Is this spread yours?"

"Just a small corner of it. My mother sold off most of the land when my father died. My brothers and I run a few thousand head with the Double Bar brand on what's left. My oldest brother, Jake, manages the place for her, in addition to his own."

Molly's store of knowledge about ranching would fit on the tip of the proverbial pin, but a few thousand head sounded like a pretty good-sized operation to her. Curious, she tilted her head to study Sam Henderson, onetime rancher, ex-Air Force Major, and currently unemployed as far as she could tell. "So why did you settle here in Vegas if you own land in Arizona?"

He hesitated a mere fraction of a moment, then lifted his shoulders in a shrug. "It's more convenient here."

Molly wondered at that brief pause, and at the deliberate casualness of his reply. Obviously, Sam Henderson didn't like talking about his past. Or was it his present that put that touch of cool reserve into his voice? More curious than ever about her mysterious neighbor, she decided to bend her self-imposed no-meals, no-mingling rule. Just for tonight.

"A steak sounds wonderful…if you're sure it's no trouble?"

"I'll fire up the grill while you get settled."

It didn't take Molly long to choose between the three upstairs bedrooms. The one at the top of the stairs obviously doubled as a study. A sophisticated computer system sat atop a desk, while the rest of the room was taken up with bookshelves and a striking hunter green leather sofa. An antique sleigh bed and a massive Korean chest in teak and brass dominated the second room. Suppressing a pang of serious envy over the beautiful chest, Molly peeked in the third room.

It had to be the master suite, since it ate up the whole back half of the second floor, but the huge room hardly looked lived in. Granted, the giant-sized bed attached to a wall unit filled with books was truly awesome. And, yes, Molly would have committed serious mayhem for the comfortable, high-backed leather chair and ottoman in one corner. Yet she didn't get a sense of sanctuary, of welcoming retreat, as she did in her own, far more sparsely furnished bedroom. Nor did she spot a single item of clothing draped over the back of the chair or tossed on the floor. Either Sam's military training had turned him into one of those disgustingly neat obsessive-compulsives, or he didn't spend a lot of time in his bedroom.

Considering the nights she'd laid awake listening to Buck Whatsisname, Molly supposed it was the latter. More curious than ever about her neighbor's nocturnal habits, she deposited her tote on the sleigh bed in the guest room and headed back downstairs. The aroma of hot, sizzling charcoal drew her to the patio.

"How do you like your steak?"

"Burned black on the outside, no trace of pink on the inside."

Molly braced herself for the usual argument. Everyone from waiters to friends to ex-fiancés... particularly ex-fiancés...gave her grief about her preference for meat cooked to the consistency of blackened shoe leather. To his credit, Sam merely winced.

"This could take a while." He forked a slab of beef a good three inches thick onto the grill. "Would you like a cold beer while you wait?"

"I don't drink beer," she reminded him with just a hint of priggishness. She hadn't completely forgotten the nasty cracks he'd made about her empty beer cans during their initial skirmishes.

"That's right." His eyes glinted above the glow of the coals. "You only wear it. How about a glass of wine, or do you only wear that, too?"

"Just on special occasions." She replied, grinning. Her gaze drifted past Sam to the dark outline of her house. Slowly, her smile evaporated. "Like when I hear things go bump in the night."

Who had made that noise? she wondered for the

gazillionth time since her meeting with Detective Kaplan this morning. Whose shadow had she seen moving along the wall? Had Joey Bennett's killer come after her, too? Was he lurking somewhere close by right now? Watching her? Waiting to get her alone? She shivered and edged a step closer to Sam.

He caught the small movement. As she had, he shot a quick look at the darkened house beyond the hedges. His chin took on a determined tilt, but his voice held only calm assurance.

"You're safe here, Molly. My security system came with a whole battery of motion-activated floodlights. I turned them on this morning. No one can get anywhere near this place without lighting it up like a Christmas tree…and answering to me."

That went a good way toward soothing Molly's jittery nerves. Settling in a springy, striped patio chair, she hooked a heel on its crossbar and wrapped her arms around her knee.

"I can't believe I got myself involved in such a bizarre situation. Brady would, though. He was always telling me that I was too impulsive, that I needed to slow down and think things through."

"Brady?"

"My onetime fiancé. I left him and most of my furniture back in Boston when I sublet my apartment and moved to Vegas six months ago."

That explained her empty house, Sam thought. It didn't explain the sudden, inexplicable kick of satisfaction he got from knowing that his quirky neighbor was currently unattached.

Or was she?

"Six months, huh?" He probed her steak with the long-handled fork, raising a chorus of spits and sizzles. "Do you still miss him?"

Her full mouth curved in a slow, impish smile that did strange things to Sam's lungs.

"I miss my couch more."

He was still trying to recover from his momentary lack of oxygen when Molly turned the tables on him.

"What about you? The first time I called here, a woman answered the phone. Is she someone special? Someone who might wonder what your neighbor is doing camped out in your guest room?"

Sam thought briefly of the sexy, red-haired intelligence officer he'd been seeing off and on before his accident. Smart, talented and ambitious, Janet Green had wanted to take their relationship to the next level. They were a perfect match, in her view. Both dedicated to their jobs, both on the fast track to the top, they understood the pushes and pulls of a military marriage.

All during Sam's long rehab, Janet had remained convinced the Air Force wouldn't put him out to pasture. He was too valuable a resource, too experienced a test pilot. She'd been shocked when he accepted without a fight the Medical Evaluation Board's ruling of a temporary retirement. She'd come by several times after he'd hung up his uniform and moved into this house, trying to understand, even offering to put her own fast-moving career and upcoming transfer to

Washington, D.C., on hold while he contested the MEB's decision.

Sam knew when and how to pick his battles. This wasn't one he intended to fight. Until he conquered the blinding pain that attacked him all too frequently, he couldn't fly, couldn't give his usual two hundred percent to any job. Hell, at times he could hardly see.

There was no way he was pulling any strings to get back on active duty. He wouldn't do that to the Air Force, or to himself. After their last argument over his decision, Janet had left, disappointed and hurt, although Sam suspected that her disappointment stemmed primarily from learning that their "perfect match" wasn't so perfect after all. She hadn't been back since.

"No," he told Molly, adding his steak to the grill beside hers. "There's no one special. Do you want to eat out here? I nuked a couple of potatoes in the microwave. I'll bring them out while these finish cooking."

"I'll get them."

She pushed out of the patio chair and went inside. Sam kept one eye on the sizzling meat and one on the swing to Molly's backside. She filled out a pair of jeans nicely, he had to admit. Very nicely.

Without warning, the memory of how she'd snuggled against him last night came rushing back. It had taken a concerted effort, but Sam had managed to keep that particular memory at bay most of the day. He'd darn well better keep it tucked away for the short time Molly would spend under his roof. He couldn't let himself think about the way her breasts had pressed against his chest. Or the neat fit of her bottom in his lap. Not if he was going to make it through the next few days without doing something stupid…like forgetting that his prickly neighbor could put out more sharp spikes than a desert cactus when she wanted to. Or that he wasn't in any condition to take up where he and Janet had left off.

No, he'd play it easy and friendly for the next few days. That approach seemed to be working well tonight. His neighbor hadn't snuck in any digs about his music or her bushes, and Sam didn't feel any aggravating curl of pain around the base of his skull. With luck, that surprisingly pleasant state of affairs would hold until Molly moved back into her own quarters.

Easy and friendly lasted all through dinner, eaten by the light of the stars and a couple of candles Molly had found in one of his cupboards.

It took them through an hour of idle, after-dinner conversation, where the topics drifted from Boston to Arizona to Vegas. From her newfound passion for the spangles and spandex so popular here, and his for the '67 Mustang he was restoring. From her current job, which Sam found fascinating, to his former one. He even opened up a bit himself, admitting that a flameout over the desert and a head-to-head with a stubborn canopy had forced him into a temporary medical retirement. When pressed, he said only that his nightly workouts were slowly getting him into better physical condition than anyone would have predicted six months ago.

Easy and friendly even got them through an awkward moment Friday morning, when Sam came downstairs to find Molly about to return to her own house. She hadn't wanted to wake him, she explained, but she had to shower and change for work.

Sam didn't bother to remind her that he'd gotten used to operating with little or no sleep...or that he'd spent half the night trying not to picture her sprawled across the bed just down the hall, and the other half wishing he could go downstairs and work off the tension that gripped his lower body when he did. He simply walked her home, checking the entire house before returning to his own.

There was nothing even remotely easy or friendly about Sam's condition late Friday night, however. His head pounded like the jackhammers heard constantly all around Las Vegas. An entire construction crew could have been riveting steel beams in there.

He prowled the darkened downstairs, desperately needing exercise but reluctant to wake Molly by pumping the clacking, clattering weights. He needed the distraction of one of Buck Randall's lonesome laments. He needed....

"Sam?"

He spun around, and the pain slam-dunked through his brain. The sight of Molly wearing a wide brown stripe across her nose and cheeks and a baggy T-shirt that dropped down to her knees didn't help his condition, either. How the hell could the woman manage to look sexy in a cotton sack?

"What do you want?"

He didn't realize he'd barked at her until she took a quick step back, blinking. She recovered before he did, her surprise morphing into concern.

"Are you okay?"

"I'm fine. Go back to bed."

Ignoring his growl, she padded into the darkened room. "What's the matter? Why can't you sleep? Why don't you ever sleep?"

"I sleep when I want to," he ground out, adding a silent "sometimes."

"Uh-huh. That's why I see lights on at your place all hours of the night."

Sam was in no mood to argue. He couldn't.

"All right. I get headaches once in a while. That's what happens when you butt headfirst through a sup-posedly shatterproof canopy."

"Have you got one now?"

"Yeah," he admitted, trying not to grind his teeth. "Go back to bed, Molly. It'll go away. They always do."

Eventually.

"Can't you take something?"

She floated toward him in the darkness, all pale, sleep-tossed hair and flaky brown facial. Above the peeling stripe laid across her upper cheeks and nose, her eyes were wide with a concern that teetered so close to pity that Sam's jaw tightened another notch.

"Didn't the doctors give you some pain pills?"

He would have snorted if he didn't know the effort would blow off the top of his head. "I've got a whole pharmacy full of pills upstairs. Every color and variety you can name."

"Tell me what you need. I'll go get it."

"No."

"But...."

"No!" His lips pulled back in a snarl. "I'll be damned if I'm going to spend the rest of my life doped up and out."

To Sam's surprise, she didn't back down. She didn't even flinch. She stood toe to toe with him, her face scrunched up under her half mask.

"So you're going to spend the rest of your life living like a vampire? Pacing through the night? Listening to that..."

She caught her breath.

"Listening to Buck Randall and pumping iron," she finished slowly. "That helps you? That...that punishment in the form of exercise? And the music?"

"Sometimes."

She frowned, dislodging a small shower of flakes. "Well, why aren't you doing either?" With a swift, indrawn breath, she answered her own question. "You didn't want to keep me awake. That's it, isn't it, Sam?"

"No."

"I've interrupted your routine, haven't I?" She searched his face, her own troubled, then spun around. "I'm going back to my own place. I shouldn't have imposed on you like this."

"Molly, wait."

He caught her arm, bringing her back around. As little as Sam wanted to spend the rest of the long hours until dawn with this splintering pain, even less did he want his neighbor alone and unprotected in her house with a killer on the loose. The stubborn tilt to her jaw told him that she wouldn't give in without a fight. Sam couldn't manage even a minor battle tonight.

"You won't help matters by going home," he said brusquely. "I'll still be awake and worrying about you."

"I'm not going to stay here and interfere with your regimen."

"Okay, okay. We'll compromise. I'll work out for a little while…"

"For as long as it takes," she insisted.

"And you stay put. Agreed?"

"Well…"

"I'll forgo Buck," he offered by way of inducement. "You pick the music."

"I have a better idea. Instead of music, why don't I just sit here and keep you company? I'll talk to you while you work out. Unless you think it would be too distracting?"

At the moment, Sam couldn't decide which was more distracting…the jackhammering in his head or Molly Duncan curled up on his couch, her long, slender legs tucked under that sexy bottom. All he knew was that he wanted to get rid of one, badly, and not the other, almost as badly. He conceded with something less than graciousness.

"Sit here then."

Stripping off his shirt, he stalked to the Universal gym and set the pin on the weights.

"Okay," he instructed, fitting his back to the bench. "Start talking."

Carrying on an easy flow of conversation in any one of several languages had never been a problem for Molly. Tucking her legs under her, she sank onto the sofa that had been pushed against the far wall to accommodate the gym.

"Have you been to the Addagio yet?" she asked. "It's gorgeous. All marble floors and tall, round columns. It's supposed to replicate the interior of a famous Venetian palace. I've never been to Venice, but if the buildings look anything like the Addagio, I have to add it to my growing list of places to visit before I die."

Sam gritted his teeth and pulled the cold steel bar down to his chest. "Where...else...is...on...your...list?"

"Don't talk," she ordered. "Just do your thing and listen. Where else do I want to go? Well, I spent a year in Tokyo on an exchange program while I was in college. I'd love to go back there again. Especially in the spring. Everyone should visit the Imperial gardens when the cherry trees blossom and a breeze catches the petals. It's like walking through a pink, perfumed snowstorm."

Slowly, Sam worked into his routine. The clanking weights took on a familiar beat. A light sweat filmed his chest and arms as they bunched, released, bunched. Even Molly's monologue seemed to pick up the rhythm, taking on a curious lilt. From her Irish grandmother, Sam guessed, his breath gusting with effort. The one with the secret recipes.

"And I want to see the pyramids," she said dreamily. "I've never been to Egypt, although I did take a side trip to Morocco once."

He could listen to her all night, he decided.

Yeah, right, an inner voice scoffed. Like listening was what he really wanted to do all night with Molly. Even with the top of his skull about to blow off, all he had to do was sneak a glimpse at his neighbor curled up on the sofa, those gorgeous legs curled under her, and he got as hard as the damned steel frame caging him in.

Grunting, Sam yanked the bar to his chest.

Molly struggled to maintain her monologue as long as she could. The clank of metal on metal had kept her wide-awake at first. Gradually, she picked up the cadence buried in the jarring sounds. Before she knew it, she was pitching her voice to match it.

Maybe she could have kept her lids up if she'd been able to see Sam's face. Or watch him as he strained and flexed his superb muscles. But they hadn't turned on a light, and he was a pale blur in the darkness.

She had no idea when she lost the battle with her

up-at-dawn, down-at-dusk internal body clock. She barely stirred when Sam slipped his arms under her and carried her up the stairs. Burying her face in the towel draped around his neck, she clung to him sleepily. The plush terry smelled of laundry detergent, she noted through a haze of weariness, and raw, elemental male. Groggy and disoriented, she nuzzled deeper into the towel. She had almost sunk back into sleep when Sam deposited her in the sleigh bed. Hovering in that hazy state of semiconsciousness, she didn't immediately react to the light kiss he brushed across her mouth.

"Good night, Molly. Thanks for the company."

The husky whisper finally penetrated. Her eyes drifted open. Sam's face hovered just inches from hers. All she had to do was lift her hand. Draw him back down an inch or two. Bring her lips to his once again.

"You're welcome," she muttered, confused and just a little stunned by the need that coursed through her.

"Sleep well."

Sure she would! Awake now and fully aroused, Molly watched him cross the darkened room to the door. It took a hard bite on the inside of her lower lip to keep from calling him back.

She wasn't ready for this, she thought in dismay. She shouldn't be fighting this sudden, urgent need to follow Sam down the hall to his own room. This greedy urge to peel off her T-shirt and take up where his kiss had left off. She shouldn't ache to slide her hands down those awesome abs. To let his powerful body crush her into the covers and...

Heat flooded her face. Her neck. Her belly.

She groaned and pulled the sheet up over her head. She had to get a grip here! She barely knew the man.

Okay, he wasn't the bloodsucking vampire or the foul-tempered martinet she once thought him. And she could have wept for the pain she'd glimpsed in his eyes when she went downstairs tonight. But Molly had learned her lesson with Brady. She'd gotten engaged to a man she thought she knew and didn't really know at all. She wouldn't jump recklessly into a relationship again.

Not that Sam showed any signs of *wanting* a relationship right now, with her or with anyone else. Obviously, he had problems of his own to work through. So did she...in the form of a nameless, faceless killer who may or may not be stalking her.

That sobering reminder was enough to push Molly into full, frightened wakefulness. She huddled under the sheet for a long while, then spent the next hour restlessly thumping the pillow and alternating between the disturbing memory of the voice she'd heard over the phone and the equally disturbing memory of Sam's lips brushing hers.

Chapter 6

As the weekend progressed, Molly tried to remember all the reasons why she should maintain some distance between her and Sam. The remembering grew more difficult with each passing daylight hour.

It got even harder at night. Sam didn't press for her company after that first evening, and Molly made sure she stayed out of his way so as not to interfere with his exercise regimen. She stuck to her plan of leaving his house early in the morning and returning late. Still, just knowing he was down the hall…or prowling the darkened downstairs, unable to sleep… kept her awake long past her normal zonk-out time.

Thankfully, the alarm company finally showed up on Monday afternoon. Sam came over to check out the system after it was installed, testing the infrared sensors and the pressure points on the stairs. Molly winced every time he set off the Klaxon. The raucous noise was loud enough to wake the entire cul-de-sac.

She moved herself and her few belongings back to her own house that night, happy to be home in a nesting kind of way. She didn't miss Sam...much. Only enough to keep her standing at the bedroom window for long moments that evening. Frowning, she stared at the light spilling through the great room windows next door. Was he hurting? Putting himself through another grueling routine? She ached for him and his lonely vigils.

On Tuesday morning, Detective Kaplan called to report that his search of the police department's database and the local pawn shops had turned up no leads to anyone with a Midwestern accent.

"So what happens now?" she asked, chewing on her ballpoint pen.

"We're going to have another chat with some of the women Joey pimped for. Talk to the bookies he owed money to. With luck, maybe one of them will give us a lead, although I'm not holding out a lot of hope. Everything okay at your end?"

"So far. No more misdirected phone calls or uninvited visitors, anyway."

"For what it's worth, I think the killer must have realized that you can't ID him. If you could, we would have tagged him by now. My guess is that he's feeling pretty secure. Assuming that was our boy you heard in the house the other night, I don't think he'll be paying you any more late night visits."

''I hope not!''

Molly hung up a few minutes later, fighting a spurt of guilty relief. She certainly didn't want anyone to get away with murder. Far from it. She'd done her part to bring Joey's killer to justice. If that wasn't good enough, well, too bad. At this point, all she wanted to do was put the whole incident behind her.

Maybe not the *whole* incident, she amended. Certainly not the spin-off truce between her and Sam.

She propped her chin in her hands, thinking about her neighbor. She still hadn't thanked him for his hospitality, and didn't have a clue how to. As she'd discovered in the past few days, Sam Henderson had narrowed his world and his focus while he battled his private demon. He seemed to have cut himself off from his past and sidestepped any talk about the future. His needs these days, he'd told Molly with a casual shrug, were simple. So what could she give this self-contained, self-sufficient man to thank him for coming to his pesky neighbor's aid?

The question had stumped her all weekend. It continued to nag at her until her idle gaze snagged on the Convention Center circular containing the printed show schedule for the week. She stared at the two-inch letters announcing a gala opening night show at Caesars Palace, then jumped up and headed for the offices downstairs.

Molly drove home that evening with the Trans Am's top down and the wind streaking through her hair. Anticipation bubbled like sparkling water in her veins. She couldn't wait to see Sam's face when she handed him the tickets nestled in her purse.

Why not just admit it? a smug little voice mocked. She couldn't wait to see Sam's face, period. So much for tiptoeing around his house and making herself scarce all weekend! The hot air rushing past her cheeks seemed to blow away all those lectures she'd given herself, all those stern reminders that she'd just escaped one uncomfortable entanglement and didn't need to fall into another. Or maybe it was Kaplan's seductive suggestion that the killer recognized he was safe, that he had no reason to come after Molly.

Whatever the reason, she felt more lighthearted than she had in days. Her resurgent spirits took a slight hit when she drove up the cul-de-sac and spotted a truck parked in the driveway next door. The red lettering on the rear panels identified the vehicle as belonging to Aqua Aruzzo Spa & Pools.

Uh, oh! Sam's pool contractor.

The Trans Am screeched to a halt halfway up her drive. Fingers drumming on the wheel, Molly stared at the truck. Had her truce with Sam ended so soon? Were they about to resume their battle over their contested property line?

The thought gave her a sinking feeling. She didn't want to redraw the battle lines. She'd gotten too close to her neighbor to paint him as the bad guy any longer. If it came to a choice between her oleanders and extending their cease-fire, she concluded with a tug of regret, her beautiful bushes would have to go.

Crunching across the lava rock between their

houses, she pressed the doorbell at the same moment the front door opened. A lanky, gray-haired stranger blinked in surprise. Just beyond him, Sam smiled a greeting.

"Hello, Molly. You're home early."

"A little. I saw the truck in the driveway. I came to talk to you about the hedge."

"It's not an issue any longer. I've asked Mr. Aruzzo to redesign the pool to leave the hedge intact."

She flashed Sam a look of surprise. "Thank you! That was very generous and…"

"Neighborly?" he suggested, his smile cranking into one of those heart-stopping grins.

"Neighborly," she echoed, trying to catch her breath. How in the world could a few crinkles at the corners of a pair of gray eyes and a crooked grin do such a number on her respiratory system?

"The new design might take some time," Aruzzo warned, climbing into his truck. "I'll have to see when our architect can get to it. With all the building in Vegas these days, we've got almost more business than we can handle."

"Tell me about it," Molly muttered.

He keyed the ignition, then added a final caveat. "With the new design, you'll have to double your laps if you're going to get the distance the docs recommend."

"I understand."

The contractor's truck backed down the drive and

roared off as Molly swung to face Sam. Dismay rushed through her in guilty waves.

"Oh, no! Why didn't you tell me the pool was part of your therapy?"

"It's not a problem."

"It certainly is! Call this guy back. Tell him to go ahead with the original design."

The dismay in Molly's eyes pierced Sam's pleasure at her unexpected appearance on his doorstep. That wasn't pity darkening them to a deep emerald, but it came too damn close for his pride to swallow in one bite. After spending a weekend in close quarters with this woman, the last thing he wanted or needed from her was pity.

Correction. He didn't *need* anything from her. But he wanted. Oh, yes, he wanted. He'd gone through six kinds of hell these past few nights knowing that she slept just a few yards down the hall from him, her face slathered with beer mush and those long legs bared to the balmy desert night. When she packed up her little plastic tote and returned to her own place yesterday morning, he'd felt relieved...and lonely for the first time in a long, long time.

He didn't like the feeling, any more than he liked the idea she felt sorry for him.

"Don't worry about the pool, Molly."

"But...."

"Let's drop it, okay? We can declare the war of the hedges officially over and done with."

She tilted her head, her frown etching deeper. The afternoon sun haloed her windblown hair. Just enough breeze swirled by to ruffle the waves even more. Deliberately, Sam blanked out the memory of how soft that tangle of silk had felt against his chin when he'd carried his sleepy guest upstairs.

"Do you want me to go with you while you check out your house?"

"No, thanks. I just saw the truck and came over to, uh...."

He forced himself to relax. "Defend your property."

"Actually," she said with a little toss of her head, "I came over to concede defeat. And I wanted to thank you again for taking me in."

"You've already thanked me. Several times."

"I know. Bear with me one more time."

Rummaging in her purse, she pulled out a small envelope and handed it to him. Sam slid his thumbnail under the flap and drew out a pair of tickets. His eyes widened at the embossed printing.

"Buck Randall's opening performance at Caesars. How the heck did you wrangle these?"

"The Center reserves a block of tickets for visiting VIPs. I strong-armed them into letting me purchase two. I know it's short notice, but I hope you can make the performance tonight."

"I can make it." He glanced down at his watch. "The show starts at nine. We've got time for dinner first."

"We?" A wave of color rushed into her face. "I didn't get you these tickets with the idea that you'd take me to the show."

Obviously not, Sam thought. He followed the becoming wash of pink from her neck to her cheeks.
Well, he'd already put one foot in it. Might as well
drop the other.

"I think you should go. What better way to learn
to appreciate Randall's artistry than to see him in
person?"

"Artistry?"

Her little hoot of derision lifted his brow. Realizing that she'd just looked her own gift horse in the
mouth, Molly hastily backpedaled.

"I'm sure he has talent."

"He does."

"I just don't have the, ah, educated ear to appreciate it."

"So it's time your ear got educated. I'll pick you
up at seven."

She hesitated, then capitulated with a smile.
"Seven it is. Let's get one thing clear, though. Dinner's on me. I still owe you for that steak."

Molly turned off the expensive new alarm system—which had set her acquisition of living room
furniture back another three months—and tossed her
purse on the hall bench. All right. She might as well
admit it. She couldn't think of anything she'd enjoy
less than sitting through a Buck Randall concert. Or
anything she'd enjoy more than spending another
evening with Sam.

She didn't even try to convince herself that she'd
accepted his invitation out of common courtesy or as

a result of his generous concession about the oleanders. Common courtesy didn't explain this pulse of excitement beating just below the surface of her skin. Sam's gracious concession hadn't generated this shivery sense of anticipation. Just the thought of being with the man for a few more hours had her quivering.

She'd been bitten by the vampire next door, she conceded, kicking her shoes in the general direction of the closet. Only time would tell how badly.

After a long, decadent bath, she dragged herself out of the tub, then debated about the proper attire for a Buck Randall concert. She considered jeans, a dressy little two-piece suit, and silky palazzo pants with a silver tank top. Finally, she settled on her favorite cocktail dress. The concert was being held at Caesars, after all.

The short, sparkly dress blazed in a sinful red. Its swishy skirt swirled just above her knees. The halter-necked bodice plunged in front and dropped even lower in back. She might not have the lush curves of a Las Vegas showgirl, Molly mused, twirling in front of the bathroom mirror, but her legs weren't bad. Not bad at all.

Piling her hair on top of her head, she secured it with a rhinestone clasp that matched the clip on her little red bag. A dab of perfume, a fresh application of makeup, and she was ready. She went downstairs to wait for Sam, hoping she hadn't overdressed for the occasion.

He rang the bell a few minutes later. Her first sight

of him resolved her doubts instantly. It also caused a minor cardiac infraction.

In casual clothes, he'd snag the attention of any female over ten or under a hundred. In more formal attire, he'd have even the post-centenarians craning around for a second or third look. He'd slicked back his dark hair. His tanned face was freshly shaven. An elegantly tailored charcoal gray suit was paired with a pale yellow shirt with a tie that splashed reds and blues and oranges in a paisley pattern. He was, Molly decided, when she gathered her stunned senses enough for coherent thought, every woman's fantasy come to life. Assuming, of course, that those fantasies ran to broad-shouldered, square-jawed, knock-you-down gorgeous males.

He flashed her a quick grin, and Molly knew she was done for.

"You look terrific."

"So do you."

"Ready to do some serious damage to your diet and your taste in music?"

Groaning, she punched in the alarm code. "As ready as I'll ever be."

She locked the door behind them, then Sam crooked an arm and led her down the walk. His gleaming, cherry red Mustang convertible waited in the driveway.

"We're going in style, I see."

"I've been working on this baby for over two years," he admitted. "Tonight's the first night I've taken her out in public. I hope she behaves herself."

"I hope so, too."

After duly admiring the restored chrome and original hood ornament, Molly slid into a leather seat that breathed saddle soap and loving hand-polishing. Her sparkly red dress swirled about her thighs before settling demurely.

Fighting to control the sudden surge of heat generated by a brief flash of leg, Sam thunked the door shut with far more force than his pride and joy deserved. And he'd thought just sleeping down the hall from his neighbor for a couple of nights was torture!

He'd needed only one look at her flushed, smiling face and throat-closing flame dress to know his torture was just beginning. Now that slither of silk stockings would thunder in his ears for the rest of the night. He didn't want to think what her light, fragrant scent would do to him.

Sam shoved the key in the ignition, realizing that he couldn't deny it any longer. He wanted her. More than he could remember wanting any woman, including the bright, ambitious redhead he'd once thought of combining careers and lives with. He might not be able to offer Molly any kind of a future, he thought with a slow twist in his chest, but he could sure give her one hell of a tonight.

Las Vegas by day could enchant the most blasé visitor. By night, it wove a gossamer, magic spell. Even after six months, Molly wasn't immune to its sorcery.

The coming dusk puffed dark clouds across the horizon as the Mustang purred its way down the cul-de-sac, behaving so well that both she and Sam were free to admire the glittering network of lights laid out below. The wind tugged her hair free of the rhinestone clip, but she vetoed Sam's offer to stop and put up the top. She didn't think she'd ever get enough of these balmy, star-studded desert nights.

Molly soon realized that Sam knew the city far better than she did. While her job had taken her to all the major hotels and tourist attractions, she hadn't yet sampled many of the small, out-of-the way places that the locals frequented. The Continental Grill was tucked away in the corner of a small strip mall and combined the best of both worlds. Its decor inside and out lacked the neon and flash of the big casino restaurants, but its menu did credit to a gourmand.

On any other occasion, Molly would have savored her chilled cucumber bisque and delicately peppered Pacific salmon and dawdled shamelessly over the cappuccino that followed. Tonight, the exquisitely flavored food and drink did little to satisfy her appetite. Sam's thigh accidentally brushing hers under the thick linen tablecloth had generated a different, far fiercer hunger. The gentle abrasion of his fingertips in the small of her back when they left the restaurant only added to it.

If she'd been a betting person, Molly would have wagered her next paycheck that three hours of Buck Randall would have killed those growing hunger pangs. Good thing she didn't. Her losses would have set the acquisition of a living room sofa back once again.

As tall and angular as he was rail-fence thin, the ex-con - turned - rodeo - stuntman - turned - recording - superstar electrified his audience with his energy. Molly still couldn't quite get past his nasal twang. Nor did she find a great deal of poetry in his lyrics, which encompassed every disaster from the death of his first love to the loss of all his worldly possessions at the hands of a devil woman named Angel. But she had to admit he threw himself into his performance and pulled everyone in the cavernous showroom in with him. His fans cheered each song. Piercing whistles accompanied each verse. Half the house belted out the choruses with him.

Even Sam got caught up in the act. Wedged next to Molly in the circular booth only a few yards from the stage, he tapped out a steady beat on her bare shoulder. At one point, his rich, deep baritone joined in the general sorrow over the theft of a piebald mare. The vibrations rumbling in his chest made Molly's nerves dance in response. She slanted a quick look sideways, her heart thumping when she observed the pleasure on Sam's strong, chiseled face. After seeing how pain had drawn it into a tight mask, she decided that Buck might just have some talent hidden somewhere under that twang after all.

She didn't really appreciate the full scope of that talent, however, until his final encore, when he pleaded with his listeners not to go to their graves without tastin' mescal or lovin' a green-eyed woman.

Sam's hand slid up Molly's neck to tangle in her hair. She turned her head to find his eyes on her. Silvery gray. Shielded by dark lashes. And hungry. So hungry her heart contracted, then exploded painfully against her ribs.

"Ever tasted mescal, Molly?"

Even with Buck amplified to forty zillion decibels and two thousand of his fans stomping feet and clapping hands, she couldn't miss the husky edge in Sam's voice.

"No."

"You've got something to look forward to then."

"If mescal is that stuff made from cactus, I don't think so."

His thumb made a slow circle on her nape. "You'll have to try it sometime. You might like it."

The applause faded to mere background noise. Buck's final refrain dimmed in her ears. Molly felt Sam's touch on her neck like a brand. Every square inch of skin that came in contact with his burned.

She didn't stop to think. Didn't try to analyze her body's response to his touch, let alone try to curb it. She leaned into him, until her breath touched his.

"Ever made love to a green-eyed woman, Sam?"

His gaze skittered, then locked with hers. For a moment, his face took on the hard edges she'd come to dread. For that same moment, Molly thought she must have misread him, misjudged the heat that rose in almost palpable waves around them.

She was searching for some bright, witty way to pass her comment off as a joke, when his face softened. A need that matched her own flared in his eyes, and he pulled her closer, nuzzling her temple.

"No, sweetheart, I haven't."

Molly melted into a puddle of bright, liquid need.

"You'll have to try it sometime," she murmured. "You might like it."

"I intend to."

Chapter 7

Consumed by the need racing through her, Molly didn't pay any attention to the whistles and shouts that erupted all around her at the end of the concert. Sam's husky promise sang in her head, drowning out every other sound.

In a shimmer of anticipation, she sat through two encores and a long, irreverent dialogue between Buck and his fans. Finally, Sam slid out of the curving booth and reached out to help her. His hand closed on hers, hard and warm, then burned a brand at the small of her back as he guided her out of the showroom and through the casino's streaming throngs.

Although it was close to midnight when they walked into the star-strewn night, Molly's inner clock hadn't sent its usual signals to shut down all systems at the first sign of darkness. Her whole body tingled with life and with an awareness of the man at her side.

She didn't want the night to end.

While Sam fished in his pocket for the valet parking ticket, Molly glanced at the brightly lit Strip. The glittering neon signs beckoned like signposts to sin. She pulsed with the urge to follow their exotic, sensual lure...but it was the display of classic roadsters parked in the semicircle in front of the casino that snagged Sam's attention.

"Would you look at that?" he breathed, riveted by a gleaming green monster loaded with chrome.

The awe in his voice made her smile. "I'm looking, but you'll have to tell me at what."

"It's a '47 Studebaker."

"I thought Studebakers went the way of the dinosaurs."

"They did." While the valet loped away to locate the Mustang in the reserved parking lot, Sam steered Molly across the circular drive for a closer look. "Before they became extinct, though, models like this one set the automotive industry on its ear. See that rear window? The all-glass notch-back caused a design revolution just after World War II."

She gave the wraparound back window respectful consideration.

"There were some protests to the radical new look, of course," Sam added with a quick, slashing grin. "The beboppers and hepcats who enticed their dates into the back seat didn't particularly appreciate the cinemascope view it gave of their activities.''

The gleam in his gray eyes caught Molly right where it caused the most damage. Her head tried to tell her that her neighbor's on-again, off-again personality had switched to full power once more. That it could just as easily switch off. Her heart wasn't buying any of it. That rebellious organ thumped erratically against her ribs, until all Molly could think of was a line from one of Buck Randall's songs. Something about slidin' down the slippery slope and not bein' able to do a damned thing to break the skid.

"In fact," Sam continued, the gleam a definite glint now, "it's my theory that every advance in automotive design pitted man's basic instincts against his baser instincts.''

"This I have to hear," she murmured as the Mustang squealed out of the underground lot and screeched to a halt before them.

Passing the attendant a hefty tip, Sam got behind the wheel. Larger-than-life statues of Greek gods and goddesses gazed serenely down on them as the Mustang flowed into the stream of traffic leaving the casino.

"Take this gearshift, for example," he said, warming to his subject. "Over time, the old, original levers evolved into a single stick shift, which in turn gave way to an automatic drive on the steering column. Far more convenient, but not as much fun as slipping the clutch and sliding this baby into gear.''

As if to illustrate his point, he maneuvered the convertible into second with an effortless partnership of hand and foot.

"Now we've come full circle. Today, every adolescent, young and old, wants a macho four-on-the-floor instead of a dull, boring automatic...and ends up cursing when the gearshift gets in his way on Saturday night."

Laughing, Molly shook her head. "Poor babies."

"You think I'm kidding?" His hand curled around the wood-grained knob. "This little gadget has been known to unman the overeager and unwary."

Somehow, she couldn't imagine Sam ever letting a little gadget like that get in his way. Grinning, she listened with mounting skepticism to his drawling recitation of the problems presented by various automotive designs on the male of the species. By the time he pulled into her driveway, his X-rated version of the evolution of bucket seats had her giggling helplessly.

"Come on! Do you really expect me to believe narrow seats are the automotive industry's counter to the sexual revolution?"

"Sure they are."

He cut the engine and slewed around with his back to the door. She shifted to give him more room, acutely aware of the way their knees knocked. Her heart was doing some knocking of its own, as well.

"Just think about it," Sam urged. "Bucket seats appeared on the scene about the same time as the

Pill. Someone had to throw a few obstacles in the path of progress.''

''Some obstacles! We're practically sitting in each other's lap.''

The glint in his eyes gave Molly her only warning that she'd walked right into that one.

''Not quite. But where there's a will...''

In one easy motion, he scooped an arm under her knees and lifted her over the offending gearshift. She landed awkwardly, her legs tangling with his and one elbow digging into the back of the seat.

''...there's a way,'' he finished smugly.

''So I see.''

Suddenly breathless, Molly attempted to extricate herself. Her elbow slipped, and she found herself wrapped tightly in Sam's arms.

For a moment neither of them spoke. Molly held her breath, wanting, aching for his kiss. He wasn't long in giving it.

This one didn't even remotely resemble the first kiss he'd given her. This wasn't any light brush of lips on lips. No casual, friendly touch of his mouth to hers. This one came down hard, and got harder.

Molly gasped, molding her mouth to his. Instant heat flared in her belly. White fire licked at her veins. She arched into him as much as her awkward position would allow, giving kiss for kiss and press for press.

She knew she was about to go up in flames when Sam buried one hand in her hair to anchor her head.

His other slid up her calf, taking the swirly red skirt with it. When his palm encountered a patch of bare flesh guarded by a lace trimmed strip of elastic, his head jerked up.

"We have to throttle back," he said raggedly. "Or take this inside."

Her stomach did a little flip. He was offering her the choice. She didn't have to think for more than a second or two.

"Let's take it inside."

He stared down at her, his face grooving with stark lines that made her stomach take another flip. Oh, no! He wasn't going to switch personalities on her now, not when she was about to melt all over his damned bucket seat.

"If you want to," she tacked on hastily.

"I want, Molly. I want so bad I hurt with it. I have since the night you came careening through the oleanders and into my arms."

"Me, too," she said simply.

Sam shouldered open the door and untangled his long legs from Molly's. Effortlessly, he reached down and gathered her into his arms. He was halfway to her front door before he thought to ask if her somewhat sparse collection of household furnishings included a bed.

"A bed I have."

By this point, Molly craved Sam's touch so badly she would have made love to him on the kitchen counter. Thank heavens for her queen-sized mattress.

She lost her dress and frilly garter belt somewhere between the front door and the upstairs hall. Still carrying her tight in his arms, Sam didn't shuck his clothes until they gained the bedroom. He dropped her on the bed with more urgency than finesse and peeled out of his suit. Molly lay sideways across the bed, her stomach hollowing when he walked toward her.

Lord, he was magnificent. Pumping all that iron had torched every ounce of fat from his body. He was rock hard, a solid mass of lean, corded muscle from his pecs to his glutes...and everywhere in between. Molly had never considered herself a connoisseur of the male physique before. A sense of humor and a keen mind rated far higher on her list of must-have qualities than a handsome face or a trim body. Now, she discovered, Sam's combination of all of the above shattered every one of her preconceived notions of raw male beauty.

On fire to touch him, she rose up on her knees. Her hands skimmed skin that felt like warm, supple leather. Entranced, she traced the expanse of his chest. The ridges and rounded slopes came alive under her fingertips, rippling at her touch.

"You almost make me want to take up exercise."

She pressed her lips to his shoulder, marveling at its smooth shape. He tangled his hands in her hair and tipped her head back. A smile sketched across his face.

"From the first day I moved in next door, you've

made me want to do a lot of things, Molly. With no 'almost' about them.''

She decided not to pursue that particular line of conversation. She didn't want to spoil the magic of the moment by careless references to run-over garbage pails or neighborly feuds. Instead, she slid her hands up and around his neck.

''What do you want to do now, Sam?''

His voice dropped to rawhide softness. ''In the words of the immortal bard, I want to make love to a green-eyed woman.''

With a silent, heartfelt *thank you!* to Buck Randall, Molly dragged Sam down. Or maybe he took her with him. However it happened, he proceeded to do exactly what he wanted. He made love to her. Slowly at first. Deliberately. Exploring every slope and valley of her body with his hands and his mouth.

No passive participant, Molly tried to match him kiss for kiss, stroke for stroke. Before either of them was ready for it, slow and deliberate couldn't satisfy the urgency that speared through them. Her panties slid down to catch on her ankle. A hair-roughened thigh slid in to press against her core. Gasping, Molly arched at the pressure. Sam used the small movement to rid her of her demi-bra. Her nipples peaked at his touch. Her breasts quivered at the scrape of his tongue and his teeth.

His mouth devoured her. Hers touched and tasted him. She was panting with need, her breasts and belly slick and aching, when Sam suddenly pulled away. The mattress rolled under his weight as he pushed himself off. Molly closed her eyes, fighting for breath, then levered herself up on her elbows. Her heart broke at the tight cast to his face.

"Oh, Sam! Are you hurting?"

His mouth twisted in a wry grin as he scooped his pants off the floor.

"I'm hurting, sweetheart. As bad as I've ever hurt in my life. Just give me a moment and we'll fix it."

The little blue package of condoms he produced banished Molly's wrenching concern. She fell back on the bed, laughing with relief. Relief gave way to singing, searing joy the moment Sam took her in his arms. When he matched his hips to hers and slid into her, she thrust up to meet him. They found a rhythm that matched their need, slow and sure at first, then harder, faster, more urgent. Pleasure centered, swirled, spread.

Sam braced himself on both elbows, determined to see Molly's face when she convulsed under him. He couldn't count the hours lately he'd envisioned her like this...head thrown back, eyes closed, face flushed with passion. Since the moment she charged through the oleanders in those skimpy purple boxers and half a T-shirt, he'd wanted her. He'd fought it. Hell, he'd pumped more iron this past week than he had at any time since the accident, and not just because of the ache in his skull.

Molly made him hurt in a way he hadn't hurt in a long time. Just the sound of her breathless little moans pushed the ache in his groin right past pain into a pleasure so intense he couldn't hold it. He thrust again, felt her slick, satiny heat grip him.

"Sam!"

She arched under him. He sank into her. The night fireballed around them.

Molly dropped into sleep with the abruptness of someone falling off a cliff. Sam wasn't surprised. He'd watched her sink into unconsciousness twice before. Tonight, she had the extra incentive of total physical exhaustion.

Smiling, he hitched her a little higher up on his shoulder. She mumbled a protest and threw an arm across his chest. One of her knees gouged into his thigh. A soft wash of breath bathed his neck.

Unlike Molly, Sam couldn't sleep. Not because his head ached, thank God. More from habit, he supposed. He'd gone so long with so little sleep, his body had accustomed itself to a lesser need.

He felt good, though. Great, in fact. The prospect of greeting the dawn without pain was joy enough. Greeting it with Molly in his arms would rank right up there among his greatest private pleasures. Better than riding out with his brothers on a cold, misty winter day to bring the cattle down from the high pastures. Even better, he thought with a grin, than the exhilaration of his first jet solo.

The grin slipped for a fraction of a second, then fixed firmly in place. For the first time, Sam didn't break out in a sweat of regret when he thought about the flying he suspected he'd never do again. He curled his arm, bringing Molly closer into his side. Slowly, deliberately, he let himself envision a future without the constant adrenaline high of the test business. Without the speed and the thrill and the edge that came with throwing high-performance aircraft across the sky.

He'd take it one day at a time, he told himself. One day at a time.

His fingers caught in the silk of her hair. He closed his eyes, breathing in her musky, womanly scent. No beer flavor this time. Not even wine or coffee. Just Molly.

The grin came sneaking back.

Maybe he'd take it one *night* at a time.

A sharp thrust to his thigh brought him jerking upright some hours later. He blinked, trying to orient himself in the dim, grayish light.

"Sorry," Molly murmured sheepishly, easing her knee away from his thigh and her bottom off the bed. "I didn't mean to wake you."

"Wake me?" Sam shook his head, still groggy. "Was I sleeping?"

"That's what it sounded like to me," she replied, her mouth curving.

"What time is it?"

"It's... Oh, no! It's after eight! I'm supposed to meet my boss at the new Visitors' Expo at nine."

She scooted off the bed and grabbed the nearest discarded garment, which happened to be Sam's shirt. As disoriented as he was, he still had time to appreciate the sight of her rounded bottom before it disappeared beneath the pale yellow cotton. He wasn't surprised when he felt his body tighten.

She turned to face him, her lower lip caught between her teeth. From the uncertainty in her eyes, Sam guessed that she was just beginning to feel the inevitable awkwardness of a morning-after.

"I have to get ready for work. Do you want to wait while I shower or, uh, do you need to get home?"

Definitely morning-after syndrome. Sam knew the cure for that. Unfortunately, he couldn't prescribe it right now. Molly had to get to work. Throwing aside the sheet, he reached for his slacks.

"You shower. I'll make coffee."

Nodding, she headed for the bathroom.

"Molly?"

She spun around, setting the shirttails to swirling and Sam's stomach to performing a full-engine stop.

"Yes?"

"I'd go to my grave happy this morning."

She stared at him blankly. Chuckling, Sam sang a few bars of Buck Randall's ode to cactus liquor and green-eyed women.

When he ad-libbed a few lines of his own that made reference to bucket seats and long-legged blondes, Molly blushed furiously and headed for the shower. She certainly wasn't ready to go to her grave this morning, happy or otherwise. Not when she felt so...so alive.

Alive and sated and the craziest bit shy. In the bright light of morning, she couldn't quite believe that she'd slept all night naked and plastered against Sam's side like wet newspaper. And that she'd taken him into her body not once, but twice. Or was it three times? She wasn't really sure, since she'd been pretty well out when he'd rolled her over and murmured certain lewd suggestions into her ear.

If those hazy memories hadn't been enough to fluster her, the sight of Sam jerking straight up in bed, the sheet barely covering his flanks, would have done it. Asleep, he'd set her pulse hammering. Awake and aroused, he'd short-circuited her entire system. And that scared her. Just a bit. Not enough to incite panic, but enough for some serious second thoughts.

Frowning, she stepped into the shower. The luke-warm water needled into her skin, sluicing away the last of her languor. Her hands impatient, she soaped her body. What the heck was her problem? Why had the sight of Sam taking up more than his fair share of her bed sent her stomach on a bumpy ride to. ..

To where?

Sam hadn't made any promises last night, Molly reminded herself sternly. He hadn't whispered any words of love in her ear.

And she didn't want any! Not yet. Not this soon.

She still hadn't fully recovered from the break with Brady. If she needed any reminders of how the wrong kind of relationship could complicate her life, all she had to do was look around her empty house. In her determination to make a fresh start, she'd left Brady *and* her Boston co-op filled of furniture.

Which didn't explain why she lingered far too long in the shower, trying to conquer the traitorous urge to call Davinia, beg out of the meeting and drag Sam back down on the rumpled sheets.

Frazzled and more than a little exasperated with her uncharacteristic doubts, Molly towel dried her hair and swiped on some blush and lip gloss. A quick search of her closet had her shimmying into a melon pink silk jersey tank dress. Tugging on its matching short-sleeved jacket and a pair of heeled sandals, she followed the mouth-watering scent of coffee down the stairs.

Sam had turned on the small TV set atop the counter, but Molly paid no attention to the too-handsome newscaster rambling on with the morning traffic report. Her every sense was tuned to the man perched on her solitary kitchen bar stool, a mug in his hands and a smile creasing his unshaven cheeks.

He'd slipped on his gray suit, minus his shirt, which now lay in a yellow pool on her bathroom floor. His colorful tie hung out of one side pocket. The combination of bare chest and tailored charcoal gabardine made a fashion statement that sent Molly's breath right back down her throat.

"Got time for coffee?"

She didn't, but Davinia would understand if she was a few minutes late. Especially when Molly confessed that she and her neighbor had finally and irrevocably ended their feud.

"A quick one," she told him, wanting to kick herself for the fluttery confusion his smile generated in the pit of her stomach. She had to get a grip here.

"Traffic's clear all the way across town," he commented as she sipped gratefully at the steaming brew. "You won't even have to navigate around any orange barrels once you get past the bulldozers and culverts at the bottom of the hill." His eyes glinted with laughter. "You can take it easy coming out of the garage."

Letting that good-natured dig pass, Molly took another swig, then set the mug aside.

"I'd better go. Davinia will be waiting for me."

He pushed himself off the stool just as the newscaster's face gave way to a platform draped with bunting. A smiling politician started to extol the values of family, work and country.

"I'll walk out with you," He reached for the off switch on the little TV. "I have to..."

"Wait!" Molly shrieked. "Leave it on!"

Sam froze, his eyes slicing from her face to the flickering screen. The handsome, prematurely gray politician smiled and waved at a cheering crowd. His voice floated out over the speakers, smooth and erudite despite the tinny amplification.

"...won't guarantee a job for every person, but the welfare reform bill I introduced last year does guarantee every person's right to a job."

The scene faded to an American flag dancing against a robin's-egg sky. An announcer urged all listeners to vote for experience and results in November. A trailer appeared, showing dates and locations of a series of public forums at which the speaker would appear.

"Th...that's him!" Molly choked out as the newscaster reclaimed the screen. "That man. That voice. That's the one I heard on the phone!"

Chapter 8

Strung as tight as wire, Sam faced Molly across the shining blue countertop. She stared at the TV, her face paper white, her eyes huge with shock. For long moments, the only sound in the kitchen came from a very competent, very pregnant weather forecaster who informed her listeners that the mercury should hit a nice, comfortable eighty-nine by mid-afternoon.

Molly's stunned gaze jumped from the TV screen to Sam. "Did you hear him? Did you see him?"

"I saw him."

"That was him!" Her voice quavered, shot up an octave. "The man who shot Joey the Horse."

"Are you sure?"

"Yes! I've heard that voice in my dreams. I recognized it instantly."

She thrust a hand through her hair and raked the

still damp waves. Her eyes locked on the TV once more. She stared at the flickering screen with a sort of fascinated dread, as if she expected the ad to repeat and the speaker to leap right out of the set.

"Do you know who that man is?" Sam asked, fighting to control his own shock.

"The banner said Congressman Somebody Walters. I've got to call Kaplan!"

Snatching up her purse, she upended it and shook furiously. A clutter of car keys, a wallet, a cellular phone in a red leather case, lipsticks, tissues, loose coins, laundry stubs and several white business cards dumped out onto the counter. Her hands frantic, she pawed through the jumble.

"Dammit, I know I have Kaplan's number here somewhere. I've got to tell him..."

"Molly, that was Congressman Joshua Walters."

Sam's flat remark pierced her absorption in her task. Her head shot up.

"So?"

He pulled in a deep breath. "So Josh Walters has represented this district in Congress for more than ten years."

"So?"

"He's well known in this area, Mol. He pushed through tough anti-crime legislation that helped clean up the Strip. He also secured tight defense department construction dollars for a new test facility at Nellis. Word has it that he was the architect for the family values platform in the last Presidential campaign."

"And that means he couldn't also pull a trigger and blow someone away? Come on, Sam, get real."

She shuffled through the jumble once more, then pounced on a card. She was reaching for the phone when Sam caught her wrist.

"I know him, Molly. I took him up for an orientation ride in an F-16 a few years ago. I shared a table with him and his wife in D.C. during the Air Force's fiftieth anniversary celebrations. I can't believe Josh Walters would have any dealings with a sleaze like Joey Bennett, let alone murder him."

Storm clouds gathered in her green eyes. She yanked her hand away with an angry twist. "Believe it or not, I know what I heard."

Sam saw that he had to tread warily here. The woman who'd flamed in his arms just a few hours ago was now shooting angry sparks at him.

"You just caught a few words of the ad," he pointed out, struggling to sound calm and reasonable. "Maybe you should listen to it again before you make any allegations against a man as powerful as Walters."

"Maybe I should," she conceded grudgingly. "So what do you suggest? That I sit around here all day waiting for the ad to air again?"

"Call Kaplan. Tell him to meet us at the TV station. We can review the clip there."

"We?" Her chin lifted. "Are you sure you want to get mixed up in accusations against your buddy?"

"He's not my buddy, but I do like and respect the man. Give me a few minutes to clean up, okay? Then we'll drive down to the Channel Five studios. If Kaplan can meet us there, fine. If not, we'll get a videotape of the clip and take it to him."

"All right."

He brushed a kiss across her rebellious mouth and headed for the patio door.

Molly watched him disappear through the oleanders. Her nerves still jumped and spit like cold grease in a hot skillet from the shock of hearing the voice that had haunted her for the past week.

She sagged a hip against the counter, willing her heart to stop skittering all over her chest. How ironic that she'd hear the killer again just when she'd decided to put him and his damned voice out of her mind. When she'd started to feel safe again, secure in her own home. Her hand trembling, she reached for the phone. To her relief, Kaplan was in the office and more than willing to meet her at Channel Five in a half hour.

Sam reappeared a few moments later, neat and composed in khaki slacks, a teal knit shirt that hugged his muscled frame, and aviator sunglasses.

"Ready?"

Nodding, she extracted her keys from the jumble, then swooped her arm across the counter to dump the rest back into her purse.

"Want me to drive?" he asked.

"No, I will."

She needed to occupy her hands or she'd start gnawing on her nails. As it was, she barely missed scraping the side of the car on the garage when she backed out. Pointedly, she refused to meet Sam's sardonic glance. The white Trans Am was down the hill and skimming past the row of concrete culverts awaiting burial beside the road at the bottom of the foothills when she suddenly remembered her meeting with Davinia.

"Damn! I forgot to call my boss."

Dragging her purse onto her lap, she dug through the jumble for her cell phone. The steering wheel, the phone, and a bulldozer rumbling across the road all vied for attention. Sam reached over and tugged the little Motorola out of her hand.

"What's her number?"

"She'll have left her place by now. Her mobile is number three on the recall."

He punched the speed dial button and held the instrument to his ear.

"Try information," Molly instructed when he got no answer. She flung a look over her shoulder and ignored the reflex stomp of Sam's foot when she swung the Trans Am off the road and up the ramp to the interstate. "Get the number for the Visitors' Expo, would you? She might already be there. Her name's Davinia Jacobbson."

When he couldn't raise an answer at the Expo offices, Sam snapped the phone shut and calmly suggested they go by and leave a message for her. The Expo Center was on the way to the Channel Five studios…and Molly was certainly making good time.

Taking his advice and ignoring his gibe, she exited the interstate onto Paradise Road. The Trans Am pulled into the Expo Center's paved lot a few moments later, right behind Davinia's coal black Jag. Her boss slid out of her car, all long, curvy legs and bright orange heels.

"Hey, girl."

"Hi, Davinia." Slamming the convertible's door, Molly hurried across the few yards of asphalt. "I tried to reach you on your car phone."

"Antonio's got it," the blonde replied.

"I can't make the meeting this morning. Something's come up."

Davinia's turquoise eyes slid past her to the man unfolding his long frame from the Trans Am.

"So I see," she purred.

Molly swallowed a groan. She wasn't ready to explain Sam. Or last night. Or her confused second thoughts this morning. When he appeared at her elbow, however, she knew there was no way of avoiding the inevitable.

"Davinia, this is my neighbor, Sam Henderson. Sam, my boss, Davinia Jacobbson."

Sam peeled off his sunglasses and held out his hand. Davinia laid her palm on his, her full mouth tipping upward in unabashed, unrepentant female appreciation.

"Welllll, welllll. Now I understand why Molly opted for sleeping with the enemy instead of camping out in my guest room."

Sam shot the red-faced Molly an amused glance but thankfully didn't let Davinia know just how accurate her comment was.

"We've called a truce," was all he said.

"So she told me." A feline smile curved Davinia's lips. "Now I see why."

Her gaze lingered on Sam's face, but Molly knew darn well she hadn't missed an inch of the rest of his tall, muscled frame. How could she? That soft knit shirt showed off every square centimeter of it. Sure enough, Davinia's smile went up another few watts.

"You'll have to meet Antonio sometime. He's into bodybuilding, too. He's also got great hands, if you're ever in need of them."

Sam looked a bit startled at that revelation, but merely acknowledged the unknown Antonio's talents with a sort of half nod.

"We just stopped by because I couldn't catch you on the phone," Molly interjected hurriedly. "I heard the killer on TV this morning, Davinia. The man who shot Joey the Horse."

"No kidding!"

"We're on our way to the TV station to listen to the news clip again. The detective in charge of the case is meeting us there."

Instant concern darkened her boss's eyes to a deep aqua. "Make sure you watch yourself until this guy is in custody, okay? Or is that why you're along for the ride?" she challenged Sam.

"That's one of the reasons."

She looked as though she wanted to explore that flat, uncompromising comment. Molly didn't give her the opportunity.

''We've got to go. I'll see you later.''

''Why don't you both see me later?'' Davinia suggested as they turned away. ''Antonio will want to hear this, too. How about my place for dinner? Around seven, if you can make it.''

''I'll let you know,'' Molly called over her shoulder.

Once back in the Trans Am, she threw Sam a quick apology. ''Sorry 'bout that. My boss can be a bit overwhelming at times. Please don't feel obligated to take her up on her invitation.''

''I don't.'' He slanted Molly a wry look. ''Before I decide one way or another, though, you'd better clue me in. Just what does this Antonio do with his hands?''

A quick smile pushed its way through her tension. ''He's a masseur. A good one, according to Davinia, and she should know. They've recently moved in together.''

''In that case, I'm game if you are.''

''I guess so.''

The noticeable lack of enthusiasm in her reply lifted Sam's brows. Obviously, she still hadn't worked her way through those morning-after, what-have-I-started-here doubts. He could sympathize with her. He wasn't sure what he'd gotten into, either. He only knew that he'd come out of the first decent night's sleep that he'd had in months with Molly's scent on his skin and the driving urge to take her flushed face in both hands and kiss her until her toes curled.

Still, he might have pulled back and let their explosive attraction take its own, natural course if that damned campaign ad hadn't put such shock in her eyes again.

Sam still couldn't believe that the sound of Josh Walters's voice had painted that stark fear on her face. Christ! Josh Walters, of all people! Half of him was absolutely convinced that Molly had mistaken the man's voice. The other half...

The other half broke out in a cold sweat at the idea that she might find herself crosswise of the congressman. *If* he had killed someone, and *if* he believed for one minute Molly could finger him, Josh would make a formidable, dangerous adversary.

She had to be wrong.

His hope that a second hearing would shake Molly's conviction died ten minutes after they arrived at Channel Five.

Al Kaplan was waiting for them in the lobby. At his request, the receptionist summoned the station manager. A tall, desiccated chain-smoker, the manager's eyes glowed with the possibility of an exclusive as he led them back to a sound booth. It took him only a few moments to cue the tape to the paid political advertisement that punctuated the morning news show.

"That's him," Molly said fiercely. "That's the man I heard on the phone. I'm sure of it."

She listened to the tape once more, her arms wrapped tight around her waist. Encased from neck to knees in a long, clinging tube of melon-colored fabric, she formed a brilliant splash of color against the racks of equipment. She also, Sam noted with a notch to his breath, looked and sounded utterly convinced. Sam saw a shiver wrack her slender frame when the congressman's voice filled the booth once again.

"Listen to the way he rounds his vowels," she instructed. "He came from the upper Midwest, I'm sure. Wisconsin. Maybe Michigan. And there! Did you catch the way he pronounces 'i-dee-ah.' That's pure New England. The congressman traveled some before he took up residence in Nevada."

"She nailed him!" the station manager exclaimed. "We've got Walters's bio somewhere here on file, but if my memory serves me, he was born in Eau Claire, Wisconsin, and graduated with top honors from Harvard. He settled in Nevada after he married Jessica MacGiver, great-granddaughter of old Jessie MacGiver."

At his listeners' uncomprehending expressions, the manager flapped a hand tipped with brown, nicotine-stained fingers.

"MacGiver was one of the early prospectors in these parts. He discovered the Blue Diamond, which turned out to be the richest silver mines in this state. One of the richest in the country, as a matter of fact. The old man's son diversified into other minerals...copper, tungsten, lithium...and made another killing. Jessica MacGiver inherited a financial empire that would make Bill Gates's pile look like play money.''

Kaplan eyed the man thoughtfully. ''You know a lot about the family.''

''I should.'' His smoke-wrinkled lips twisted. ''MacGiver, Inc., owns this station, plus a half dozen newspapers around the state.''

''I bet the congressman doesn't pay much for his political ads,'' Molly muttered.

The manager re-cued the tape, his pallid eyes zinging from the politician's handsome face to her taut one. ''What's Walters done, anyway?''

''We don't know that he's done anything,'' Kaplan responded evenly.

''Come on,'' the newsman huffed. ''What gives? Are you investigating him for illegal campaign contributions? Misuse of government aircraft?''

''Not at this time, and if I were you,'' Kaplan added laconically, ''I'd be real careful about mentioning our visit here. To anyone. I doubt if Mrs. Walters would appreciate it if one of her employees started unfounded rumors flying about her husband.''

With that unsubtle hint, the detective lifted the tape off the mixer. ''I'll take this, if you don't mind.''

''No, no, of course not.''

After the controlled dimness of the TV station, the blazing morning heat hit Molly like a hammer. She stepped into the searing sunlight, half blinded and wholly shaken by the idea that she might have just identified a member of one of the most powerful families in her adopted state as a murderer.

"What do we do now?" she asked Kaplan, sliding on a pair of oversized sunglasses to shield her eyes from the shimmering white light.

He rubbed his hand across his jowls, his black eyes thoughtful. Obviously Molly's disclosures had had more of an impact on him than he'd let on inside the production booth.

"I'll check out Walters's whereabouts on the night of the murder," he said slowly. "I'll also see if there's any record that he owns a .38 special. I'll get back to you with whatever I find out."

Molly nodded, both disappointed and secretly a little relieved. While she wanted Walters brought to justice, she wasn't looking forward to what came next. She wouldn't mind taking a few days or weeks or even months to get over her jitters before she had to face the politician across a courtroom.

Kaplan started to turn away, then swung back. "Look, Ms. Duncan, you've convinced me that it could have been Walters you heard on the phone that day."

She anticipated the "but" before it came.

"The thing is, the D.A. won't press the case against him without some hard, corroborating evidence."

"And you don't think you'll find that corroborating evidence, do you?"

"No. Number one, a man like Walters is too smart to leave any. Number two…"

"Yes?"

"I've spent some twenty-three years on the Las Vegas police force. During those years, I've seen supposedly upstanding citizens commit crimes that turned even my stomach. Yet I've never heard any snitch or undercover cop even whisper the congressman's name in conjunction with anything off-color. No gambling debts, no under-the-table donations to his campaign, nothing."

"So what are you suggesting? That I forget what I heard? Or lie about it?"

"No, of course not. I'm just suggesting you keep quiet until I have a chance to check Walters's whereabouts the night of the murder, that's all. This case has the potential to get real nasty, real fast."

"Thanks for the warning...I think."

The detective shrugged and left with another promise to call when and if he turned up any information.

"Why the heck am I starting to feel like the guilty one here?" she muttered to his back.

She slumped a hip against the Trans Am's fender. Instantly, hot metal seared through her dress. With a short, pithy oath, she leaped away from the fender and smacked into Sam. He steadied her, his face tight behind the aviator glasses.

"Don't you start, too," she warned, pulling free.

She slid into the white convertible, wincing when the baked seats came in contact with the backs of her thighs. A quick twist of the key overcranked the engine, which in turn caused Sam to wince. Feeling even more disgruntled than she had when she slipped out of his arms and headed for the shower earlier this morning, Molly threw him an accusing look.

"I know this Walters is a friend of yours."

"An acquaintance."

"Whatever." Shoving the convertible into reverse, she wheeled it out of the parking slot. "I don't need you to remind me again that I only heard him for a few seconds. Or how powerful he is."

"I hadn't planned to."

"And I don't need anyone telling me that whole thing is going to detonate like a nuclear device when the media gets hold of it."

"No, you don't." He slid his sunglasses down his nose and returned her glare. "Would it do any good to remind you that I'm not the responsible party here, either?"

"You're just as responsible as I am," she shot back.

"Come again?"

Molly knew she was being unreasonable. She recognized that her emotions were riding a towering crest from last night and this morning. Still she couldn't hold back a snide little reminder.

"If you hadn't been inflicting Buck Randall on me night after night, I wouldn't have called to complain, I wouldn't have heard a shooting, and I wouldn't be about to finger a U.S. congressman for murder."

Yeah, Sam thought. And I wouldn't be having dinner tonight with the divine Davinia and her masseur, instead of locking Molly's front door, dragging her down onto the nearest horizontal surface, and kissing her until her bones rattled, which was the only way he could think of at the moment to shake her out of her present snit.

Shoving his glasses back up the bridge of his nose, he tucked his arms across his chest. This was going to be a long day. And an even longer night.

Chapter 9

By the time Molly dropped Sam off at his place and got back to her office at the visitors' bureau, she'd recovered some measure of her equanimity. Thankfully, Davinia hadn't yet returned to the office. Molly's timely meeting with a German trade delegation at the Excalibur Hotel and Casino won her a further reprieve from the third-degree she knew her boss would subject her to.

After the lengthy meeting at the Excalibur, she dialed her voice mail to check her messages. Her stomach knotted when she heard Detective Kaplan's voice asking her to call him as soon as possible. When she reached him at his office, he cut right to the point.

"Walters has an airtight alibi for the night of the murder. He and his wife were the guests of honor at a fund-raiser at the Mirage. According to my sources, the governor, some two thousand assorted well-heeled contributors and an entire galaxy of Vegas's resident entertainers attended the bash.''

Caught between relief and an instinctive need to refute the evidence, Molly stared through the plastic shield of the phone booth at Excalibur's version of the haunted forest outside Camelot. Moss draped from shadowy overhead limbs, and a gray-bearded Merlin wandered the black-and-red carpeted floor, hawking puppets to a group of shy, smiling Japanese tourists.

''What time did the fund-raiser end?'' she asked, frowning at Merlin.

''According to my sources, the entertainment ran longer than anticipated. The party started to break up just past one, but Walters and his wife lingered until most of the guests departed the scene. I've verified that he was at the Mirage until 2:00 a.m.''

''The shooting occurred just after one,'' Molly murmured.

''We're still checking the gun records, but it doesn't look like the congressman is our killer.''

''No,'' she conceded slowly, ''it doesn't.''

Molly hung up a moment later. Doubt swarmed inside her head like annoying little gnats. She would have staked everything she owned on the certainty that she'd heard Joshua Walters at Joey the Horse's apartment. Unless the congressman had a twin or he'd taken a few lessons from Sigfried and Roy in magic and illusions, she must have heard wrong.

She was still puzzling over the question of how

Walters could have been in two places at the same time when she drove home a little past five that evening. The sight of the garage next door yawning open and Sam bent over the fender of the Mustang pushed the congressman to the periphery of her mind. Instant, deliciously carnal thoughts leaped to center stage.

Okay, she told herself as Sam unbent. All right. The dizzy loop her stomach just performed was perfectly natural, a normal, healthy woman's response to those thigh-hugging jeans and that stretch of white T-shirt across his broad chest. She didn't have to panic. She wasn't in love with him or anything. Only in lust.

Very much in lust, she admitted as he wiped his hands on a rag. She braked the Trans Am to a halt, waiting while he crossed the driveway. His dark brown hair gleamed with sweat at the temples, and the damp patches on his T-shirt had Molly's hands clenching on the steering wheel. But it was his face that twisted her heart.

His cheekbones jutted in stark relief, stretching his tanned skin into a thin membrane. His mouth formed a narrow slash. And his eyes... Molly could have cried at the tight, white lines fanning from their corners.

"Bad day?" she asked softly.

"I've had worse."

The clipped response warned her that he didn't want any sympathy. That and the hard line to his jaw.

"I talked to Kaplan a while ago," she said, burying her ache for Sam in the casual information. "Your friend Walters was the guest of honor at a fund-raiser the night of the murder. He didn't leave the gala until an hour or so after the shooting."

His expression didn't soften. If anything, it torqued up another degree. He was hurting, Molly knew. Badly. Her heart twisted for him.

"I won't say that I'm not relieved," he told her. "Josh Walters has done a helluva lot for this state and for the country. I like the man. I didn't like the idea that he's a murderer."

"I don't particularly like it, either. Look, Sam, do you mind if we take a rain check on dinner with Davinia and Antonio? We, uh, didn't get much sleep last night and I'm whipped."

He skimmed her face with tight, shuttered eyes. Heat rose in her cheeks. She didn't know which was worse. Remembering the strenuous activities that had precluded sleep last night or letting Sam believe that she didn't want to repeat them.

She did, she acknowledged. With every hormone in her body. But not until she'd worked through her own confused reaction to this man. And certainly not until he could look at her without pain gouging deep grooves on either side of his mouth.

"I'll call Davinia and beg off. She'll understand."

That was the understatement of the week. Her boss would not only understand, she'd put her own spin on things. No doubt she'd chuckle evilly and remind

Molly that she and Sam needed to come up for air
sometime.

Sam cocked his head slowly, as if wary of moving
too fast. "Backing off, Molly?"

"A little," she admitted, sliding her hands back
and forth on the steering wheel. "I think we might
need to slow things down."

"Why?"

The simple question demanded the truth.

"I rushed into one relationship and ended up
couchless." Her smile invited him to understand. "I
don't want to rush into another one with a man I was
about to declare all-out war on a week ago. Let's
take this slow, Sam, and see what develops."

Sam told himself that she was right. Between the
sharp spikes shooting into the back of his skull, he
acknowledged that it wouldn't hurt to slow things
down just a little. The problem was, he was afraid
he'd gone beyond slow. He'd passed that point at
Caesars Palace, when he'd glanced across the booth
and watched Molly pretend to enjoy an art form she
despised. Or maybe when she giggled helplessly and
collapsed against him in the driver's seat of the Mustang. For sure when she shimmied and shivered and
welcomed him into her body.

Sam had spent most of the day thinking about
what he wanted from and with Molly Duncan, and it
wasn't slow. All morning he'd tried to figure out how
to shield her from the ugliness of this damned murder, which could have gotten even uglier real quick.
A good chunk of the afternoon went to wondering

just how she'd take to being shielded, from murder or from anything else.

Then the first distress signals had started. Low in his skull. Blunt at first. Gradually sharper and sharper. He'd worked out on the gym until his muscles screamed. Finally, he'd buried himself in the dim sanctuary under the Mustang's hood. Now, he fought to keep a rusty edge from his voice as he forced himself to agree with Molly.

"You're right. Maybe we'd better back off for a while." His mouth twisted in what he hoped was a smile. "For tonight, anyway. See you."

Molly couldn't let him walk away like this. Shoving the Trans Am into park, she pushed the door open and slid out.

"Sam! Wait."

He swung back to her, so stiff and taut he might have been carved from stone. Lava rock crunched under her soles as she closed the short distance between them. Her heart aching, she laid a hand on his arm.

"Would it help if I came over for a while? I could talk to you while you work out."

The muscles under her fingertips flinched. His eyes turned to slate.

"No, thanks."

"Sam, I can see you're hurting. Let me help. As a friend...or a pesky, interfering neighbor, if nothing else."

He hesitated, then lifted a hand to cup her cheek. His thumb brushed her lower lip.

"Thanks for the offer, neighbor, but you look as whipped as I feel. Get some sleep, then we'll take this discussion up where we left off."

The way his thumb teased her lip suggested that they'd take up more than the discussion. The kiss he dropped on her mouth confirmed it.

Molly watched him bury himself under the hood of his toy again. Feeling more confused than ever, she reclaimed her car and hit the garage opener. The door rumbled up, then down, closing out the slanting desert sunlight, the heat and Sam Henderson.

Five hours later, she blew out a long, irritated puff of air and let the bedroom shade drop.

Dammit! Sleep pulled at her like a high-powered magnet. The nest she'd made in the bedcovers sang out her name. She needed sleep. She craved total oblivion.

Even more, she craved the man next door. Her head could enumerate every reason why she should stick to her determination to put some space between them. Her body refused to listen to them. Her heart... Well, her heart bled every time she climbed out of bed and padded to the window to check the light spilling out of Sam's great room window.

She sank down into the nest again. Drawing up her legs, she plopped her chin on her knees. The facial slathered across her nose and cheeks cracked a bit. A flake or two drifted down to settle on the pale green duvet.

Sam didn't want her hovering over him. He'd

made that clear enough. He didn't even want her talking to him. As grim as he'd looked earlier, he probably didn't even want to...

The shrill ring of the phone had her jumping half out of her Syracuse University sleep shirt. She waited until her breath returned, then reached across the covers to snatch up the receiver.

"Hello?"

"I saw your light. Are you all right?"

Sam's deep drawl sent a slide of relief through Molly. He sounded less strung out, almost relaxed.

"I'm fine," she murmured, hugging her knees. "I just couldn't sleep. How about you? Are you okay?"

"Not quite okay, but better than before."

"I'm glad," she said simply.

A small silence spun out between them, easy and companionable. The sexual tension was still there. It simmered just below the surface, like a rich, bubbling broth just removed from the burner. A layer of the friendship Sam had rejected earlier lay atop it right now. Molly had to admit the sex was better, much better, but this would do nicely.

He broke the stillness first. "Josh Walters's campaign ad came on again earlier this evening. I taped it, and watched it while I worked out."

"And?"

He hesitated. "And I remembered a small incident, nothing significant, but it got me thinking."

Molly sat up, her pulse quickening. "What kind of an incident?"

"Remember I told you I took the congressman up for a flight a few years ago?"

"I remember." A dry note crept into her voice. "As I recall, that came up right after you all but accused me of hitting the Coors again for suggesting Walters could be a murderer."

"Yeah, well, that might have been when it was."

Molly settled for that almost-apology. "So what was this incident you remembered?"

"I didn't see it," he cautioned. "I only heard about it second or third hand."

"Okay, okay, I got the picture." She scrunched up her nose impatiently, dislodging a small storm of brown flakes. "What happened?"

"Walters hit on one of the lieutenants at the base."

Molly shoved her knees under her and surged upright. "No kidding?"

"I shrugged the story off at the time because..."

She jumped in, excited and indignant. "Because you couldn't believe your paragon of virtue, your defender of truth, justice and the American way could step off the narrow path of righteousness."

"Because the lieutenant in question is well known around the squadron for her ability to lay a first-class lip lock on the unsuspecting and unwary," he finished dryly.

"Oh!" Chagrin and curiosity fought a short, fierce battle. Curiosity won. "Did she lay one on you, Sam?"

Molly could have sworn she heard him grinning.

"We're talking about Josh Walters here," he reminded her. "I thought I'd go out to the base tomorrow and, uh, feel this lieutenant out a little more."

She refused to rise to that obvious bait. "Let me know what you find out."

"I will." His voice dropped to a slow, rough caress. "'Night, Mol."

"'Night, Sam."

With the sun beating down mercilessly from a cloudless sky and the dust from a fitful breeze stirring lazy swirls across the desert, Sam drove out to Nellis Air Force Base the following afternoon.

Located eight miles northeast of Las Vegas, the sprawling military reservation covered more than eleven thousand acres. In addition to the base proper, restricted test air space ate up another three million acres of desert, with five million more set aside for shared use with civilian aircraft. One of the busiest air facilities in the world, Nellis was home to the Air Warfare Center, the USAF Thunderbirds, and a host of composite strike forces containing Army, Navy, Marine and Air Force elements. Sam felt its pulsing vitality the moment he drove through the front gate and returned the guard's snappy salute.

The forest green Blazer he drove every day in lieu of his cherished Mustang slowed to a crawl, its powerful engine growling a protest to the base's twenty-five mile per hour speed limit. Behind the row of tan-and-brown hangars, twin-tailed jets thundered down the runway and streaked into the air. The gut-wrenchingly familiar scent of jet engine exhaust drifted across the shimmering afternoon heat. Sam drew it into his lungs like another man might the scent of a woman.

He swung off the main boulevard and headed for the maintenance complex in an isolated sector of the base, where First Lieutenant Patricia Donovitch supervised a crew of highly skilled munitions handlers. After a long drive along the perimeter road, Sam pulled up at the gate to the restricted area and waited while the guard put in a call to the lieutenant.

The young security guard returned a moment later to inform him that she'd be with him as soon as her crew finished loading a batch of missiles. Sam climbed back in the Blazer and stretched out his legs. He squinted through his gold-framed sunglasses at the F-15 soaring into the sky at the far end of the runway. From this distance, the fully armed fighter seemed to move at a slower speed than the six hundred miles an hour Sam knew she was capable of.

He waited, mentally bracing himself for the kick to the gut he knew was coming. It slammed into him just as the sleek, twin-tailed jet spiraled into a sky so vast and so blue that a poet might describe it as a playground for the gods.

Christ, he missed it. All of it. Strapping himself into a cockpit and hearing the first whine of the engines revving. Wing tips tilting into the face of the sun. The soaring climb and dizzying drop. The brotherhood of arms, stripped to its barest essentials. Even the endless flight safety briefings and boring staff meetings. Would he ever get back to it?

The F-15 disappeared into a puffy white cloud, and Sam admitted the truth.

He wouldn't be climbing back into a cockpit in the foreseeable future. It was time he accepted that fact and got on with the rest of his life.

He was still sprawled in the Blazer, staring through the open window at the puff of cloud, when a dusty maintenance vehicle passed through the gate and pulled up nose-to-nose with the Blazer. Pat Donovitch spilled out, cheerful, bubbly, and packing her own load of lethal armament under her baggy battle fatigue shirt, Even with her thick curls stuffed under a navy ball cap and her feet encased in dusty web boots, she exuded an earthy sensuality that had made her so popular at the Officers' Club on Friday and Saturday nights.

"Hey, Major Henderson. How's the head?"

Sam shouldered open the Blazer's door. "Still there, Donovitch. How're you doing?"

Her lively face twisted into a wry grimace. "As well as can be expected with Red Flag kicking off in two days. You remember how that is."

"Yeah, I do."

Sam shoved aside vivid memories of those grueling training exercises when the "red" forces assigned to Nellis attacked and tried to prevent "blue" forces—U.S. and NATO units from all over the world—from penetrating their target. The simulated air battles in the skies over southern Nevada honed the Air Force's fighting edge and wrung every last ounce of emotion and energy from all participants, air crews and support personnel alike.

"I know you're busy, Pat. I won't keep you. I just wanted to ask you about Josh Walters."

"Congressman Walters?"

Sam caught the surprise that flickered in her blue eyes, followed instantly by a shadow of wariness. Her bright, cheerful smile dimmed. He hooked a thumb in his jeans, trying to think of any way to wrap the next question up in clean linen. There wasn't any.

"I remember hearing your name linked to the congressman's a year or so ago. I know it's none of my business and you can tell me to go to hell if you want to, but I need to know if there was anything more to that rumor than squadron scuttlebutt."

The lieutenant's face lost all trace of its former open friendliness. "You're right, Major. It's none of your business. Look, I have to go. We've got another load of SAMS to arm and..."

"I wouldn't ask if it wasn't important."

His quiet comment cut through her tumbled excuses. Even more wary, she threw him a nervous glance. "Important how?"

"A friend of mine thinks she heard Walters's voice in connection with a crime."

"What kind of a crime?"

It was Sam's turn to hesitate. He was reaching here, really reaching. He didn't want to start rumors flying around the base, or slander a man he'd always respected. Yet he couldn't discount Molly's on-target identification of Walters, any more than he could dismiss this sudden reluctance to talk on the part of a young woman not particularly known for her reticence.

"A man was murdered a week ago, a small-time drug dealer and occasional pimp."

"Murdered!"

Donovitch sucked in a quick breath. Under the bill of her ball cap, her face went stark white.

"There's no proof that Walters was involved," Sam said quickly. "I just came out to talk to you on a hunch. What can you tell me about the man?"

The lieutenant rubbed her palms down the sides of her fatigue pants. She looked everywhere but at Sam.

"Not much. He came through on a tour of our facilities and sort of, well, singled me out. He asked me what I thought about women in combat, and I got in a few good shots before his handlers hustled him off."

Sam kept his voice even. "Rumor has it he did more than just single you out during his tour."

"Yeah, well, he called me."

"At work?"

"At home."

Obviously on edge, she drew a line in the sand with the toe of her boot. Sam waited, his own edginess growing by the second.

"He said he wanted to hear more on my views about women warriors," she continued slowly, reluctantly. "He suggested that we have dinner. He also suggested that I keep it quiet, as the Air Force wasn't exactly pro-women-in-combat at the time, but, well, I was flattered. I guess I mentioned the call to a friend or two.''

That's all it would take, Sam knew. The jungle beat would pick up that juicy morsel instantly and broadcast it all across the base. Donovitch confirmed his supposition with a disgusted shake of her head.

''Somehow word of the call got back to the General. From there, the tale shot straight up the chain to the Legislative Liaison office at the Pentagon.''

''Ouch!''

''Ouch doesn't begin to describe it. The air staff went bananas. Some poor captain was even tasked to prepare issues papers for me to use in discussions with the congressman. My commander passed them to me with instructions to make sure that I understood the official Air Force position. God, what a mess!''

There was more. Sam heard it in her voice. Saw it in the way her gaze slid sideways and fixed on the scrub beside the road.

''What did Walters have to say about the whole thing?''

Still she wouldn't look at him. ''Publicly, he dropped it right in my lap. In that easy, cultured way of his, he implied that the little lieutenant had her own agenda about women in the military and was certainly going to extreme lengths to press it.''

''And privately?''

She hesitated so long Sam didn't think she'd answer. Finally, she lifted her face. Defiance and an unmistakable note of fear threaded her voice.

"Privately, he called me at home again and warned me to keep my mouth shut. If I didn't..." She swallowed. "If I didn't, he had friends who would make me sorry...even sorrier than the last whore who tried to embarrass him."

The Blazer churned up a trail of dust. Sticking to the speed limit more by instinct than by conscious effort, Sam tooled the vehicle along the perimeter road. He barely noticed the two-ship flight of fighters lifting off at the end of the runway. The past no longer pulled at him. His whole being was focused on Molly Duncan and the immediate future.

His eyes slitted behind his sunglasses, Sam put Lieutenant Donovitch's short, bitter tale through a dozen different spins. With every twist and tumble, his lingering doubts that Molly had pegged the right man as the killer lessened and his uneasiness grew.

Damn! Josh Walters! Sam's knuckles whitened on the leather-wrapped steering wheel. Most of Nevada believed the congressman would breeze into the governorship after his next term in the House of Representatives. Even now, he was being touted as a possible presidential candidate after a stint as governor. Street-smart and highly educated, Walters possessed the necessary charm to propel him right to the top. The fact that he'd married into big money certainly hadn't diminished his prospects, either. He was a shoo-in for re-election and a luminous political future...unless a stubborn, green-eyed blonde with an ear for accents and a splatter of freckles across her nose fingered him for murder.

The skin at the back of Sam's neck tightened. The thought of Molly standing in Josh Walters's way to the governorship and perhaps the presidency made his pulse skitter and stop, then restart with a kick.

He took a quick look at the functional, stainless steel watch strapped to his wrist. He'd head downtown and talk to Kaplan, he decided. Then he'd wing by the Las Vegas Convention Center and see what time Molly got off work. Maybe he'd wait and follow her home. They might even, he thought with a sudden, swift stab of need, pick up where they'd left off yesterday, before Molly's morning-after doubts and Josh Walters's campaign ad had complicated matters considerably.

It was only after he'd left a thoughtful Detective Kaplan that Sam realized his protective instincts had kicked into overdrive. Keeping his pesky, irritating, seductive neighbor in his bed for the foreseeable future now ranked a distant but compelling second to keeping her safe. He was still thinking about his priorities when he pulled into the parking lot that skirted the visitors' bureau. He spotted Molly's sporty white Trans Am a few moments later...at almost the same time he spotted a hulking figure in a black collarless shirt and gray sharkskin suit jimmying the lock on her car door.

Chapter 10

"**W**hat the hell?"

With a squeal of brakes, Sam whipped the Blazer into park. He lunged out of the vehicle and across the asphalt at the same moment the individual bent over the Trans Am spun around.

If Sam had harbored any doubts about the man's intentions, the way he dropped into a fighter's crouch resolved them instantly. He was big, a real bruiser, and a street fighter. Sam didn't know whether he carried a weapon, but if he moved one of his hands a half inch toward his ankle or the inside of his suit coat, Sam would push his face into the asphalt. He approached slowly, keeping those huge, balled fists in his line of sight while he held the gorilla's gaze with his own.

"You want to tell me why you're trying to get in this car?"

Under a cap of glistening black curls, the intruder's narrowed eyes took his opponent's measure.

"Perhaps I shall tell you...if you tell me of what business it is to you?"

Sam didn't have Molly's ear for accents, but even he could tell the bruiser didn't hail from around these parts. What's more, someone had hand-tailored his double-breasted jacket to make it lie so smoothly over those bulging biceps. The suit must have set its wearer back a thousand bucks or more.

The realization that he wasn't dealing with a local punk raised the hairs on the back of Sam's neck. A dozen possibilities rifled through his mind, not the least of which was that Josh Walters had hired some big-time muscle to take care of Molly. The lieutenant's disclosures had planted more than a seed of doubt, he realized grimly. Adrenaline shooting undiluted through his veins, he curled his hands into fists.

"It's my business," he growled, "because I say it is."

"I think, perhaps, I do not like this way you talk with me."

"Tough."

"Tough?"

The curly-haired behemoth chewed on that for a moment. When he'd finished ruminating, delight sprang into his calf brown eyes.

"You wish to have the fight with me? *Bueno!*"

It didn't look too *bueno* from where Sam stood. The intruder outweighed him by some twenty or thirty pounds and had arms like giant sequoias. Sam had survived four older brothers, though, and every self-defense and escape and evasion course the Air Force had to offer. He knew how to fight dirty.

"We are of a size, you and me!" the brawny man exclaimed. "Only wait while I take off this so wonderful coat which Davinia has bought for me. Then we shall have the sport, yes?"

While his eager opponent attacked the two buttons on his sharkskin jacket, Sam eased out of his own half crouch.

"Davinia bought you that suit? Davinia Jacobbson?"

"Yes, she is most generous." Still smiling, he flexed an Olympic-sized set of muscles under the collarless black silk shirt. "I have not had the sport since I come to this country. Do we follow the rules, or do we most simply see who goes down first?"

Blood still rushed through Sam's veins at the speed of sound. The worry that had built during the drive in from Nellis and spiked right off the charts when he'd spotted this hulk fiddling with the door to Molly's car still knotted his gut. He craved an outlet for his tension, had pumped himself for knuckle-splitting violence, but a free-for-all with Davinia's lover in the Convention Center's parking lot wasn't the release he was looking for. He was about to tell the man so when a scolding feminine contralto floated across the parking lot.

"Hey, sweetcakes, you promised to get the car opened and the air-conditioning going before Molly and I…"

The svelte blonde halted, her turquoise eyes widening in undisguised pleasure.

"Hel-lo, Major. How convenient! Molly just called your place to see if you wanted to cash in that rain check you took last night. I see you've met Antonio."

"Not officially," Sam drawled.

"You are friends? You and Davinia?"

"He's Molly's neighbor," the blonde put in. "Major Sam Henderson."

"The one she fights with, then does not fight with?"

"Something like that."

He put out a hand, which the curly-haired Hercules regarded with undisguised disappointment.

"So, we do not have the sport?"

"Maybe next time," Sam replied, trying not to wince as his almost-opponent ground his bones together.

Molly's boss wrapped both her hands around her lover's arm and rubbed up against it like a cat.

"Can you join us, Major? We just finished the teleconference from hell and decided to let 'Tonio treat us to margaritas at the Hard Rock Cafe. Molly's on her way down. She'll want to hear about your trip out to Nellis. So do I, incidentally."

Sam fought to keep a frown from sketching across his brow. "She told you about that?"

"About Josh Walters, you mean?" Davinia waved a perfectly manicured set of nails. "She was pretty closemouthed about his identity at first, but I spent a few years as an attorney in a former life. I broke her down during cross-examination."

Before Sam could react to that, she organized matters with cool efficiency.

"Oh, good. Here comes Molly now. 'Tonio, you drive her car. I'll take mine, and she can go with the Major."

"I could not open the door of Molly's car," Antonio confessed with a shamefaced look. He uncurled his beefy paw to display a key ring. "I had not the right key."

"It's this one, sweetie. This one."

With a kiss that left her lover grinning foolishly, Davinia informed her surprised employee that they'd see her and Sam at the Hard Rock and climbed into her own two-seater Jaguar.

Molly looked from the Jag to the departing Trans Am to the Blazer planted sideways across three parking slots, its engine humming. Her brows lifting, she turned to Sam.

"Did I miss something here?"

"Almost."

Still pumped from his near brawl, Sam shoved a hand through his hair. He couldn't remember the last time he'd felt this kind of twisting, mounting tension. He had to get himself under control.

The sunlight painting Molly's hair to a nimbus of gold waves didn't help matters, either. Nor did the long, silky legs displayed to perfection under the thigh-skimming, hip-hugging tube of bronze knit that passed for a dress. How the hell did she bend over in that thing without getting arrested?

The puzzle presented all kinds of interesting solutions. With a wrench, Sam pulled his thoughts from acrobatics to actualities.

"It seems we're going to the Hard Rock Cafe."

"So I gathered." She accompanied him to the Blazer. "What are you doing at the Convention Center, Sam?"

"I was out at the base and came by to..."

To what? To report on his conversation with Lieutenant Donovitch? To counter the uneasiness that was knifing into him a little deeper with each passing hour? To satisfy a pressing need to keep this woman safe?

"To talk to you," he finished with a shrug. "And to Davinia, apparently."

He'd forgotten Molly's keen ear. Picking up on the underlying criticism in his offhand comment, she shot him a quick look.

"Do you have a problem with talking to Davinia?"

He had a big problem with it if the conversation resulted in the same kind of brushfire that Pat Donovitch's casual comment had sparked on base. Or the same threat to Molly.

"Kaplan's kept the station manager at Channel Five on a tight leash," Sam pointed out. "He doesn't want to spook the congressman or send the media into a feeding frenzy unless or until he's got something concrete to work with. I just hope Davinia can keep this between herself and sweetcakes.''

"She can," Molly retorted, flicking the man beside her an irritated glance.

She wasn't about to admit that she hadn't intended to spill every detail to Davinia. She'd tried, she'd really tried, to follow Kaplan's advice and keep the identity of the killer to herself for the time being. Dodging Lawyer Jacobbson's barrage of questions required far more stamina and skill than Molly possessed, however.

Of course, telling Davinia all also meant telling Antonio when he stopped by the office a while ago, but both parties had promised to keep the stunning revelation to themselves. Molly was sure she could trust them to hold to that promise. Sam, evidently, had his doubts.

She slanted him another quick glance. What was with him this afternoon, anyway? He didn't have that tight, white-lipped look that signaled one of his headaches, but his voice had a rough edge she hadn't heard since the night she sent the police to his house. He gripped the wheel with a curled fist, and his long, contoured body radiated a coiled tension. Molly had the sense of a sleek predator held rigidly in check. Quiet. Powerful. Deadly.

"What did you find out at Nellis?" she asked in an attempt to bridge the prickly silence.

His jaw notched. In an even voice that didn't quite match the sudden gridwork of lines at the corner of his mouth, he related his short conversation with Lieutenant Lip-Lock, as Molly had privately tagged her.

She was still trying to grasp the ramifications of the lieutenant's sobering story when Sam ushered her into the Hard Rock Cafe.

A symphony of sounds greeted them. Bruce Springsteen poured from speakers mounted on every wall. Early happy hour patrons shouted to be heard over the pounding beat. Glasses clinked, waiters called in orders, and Davinia hailed them from a back booth.

Weaving her way through the noise and an assortment of rock-and-roll memorabilia that included platinum records, leather jackets and Bill Haley's motorcycle, Molly felt a momentary preference for Buck Randall's softer, if somewhat more nasal ballads. It faded, thank goodness, almost instantly. Over frosted margaritas and a gargantuan platter of green chili and chicken nachos, Sam related the gist of his conversation with the lieutenant. Davinia's eyes gleamed.

"So despite his squeaky-clean record and well-publicized family life, our boy has a history of hitting on nubile young women. This opens up all kinds of interesting possibilities."

Molly swirled the straw through her slushy margarita. She'd had time to think of a few possibilities, too, and she wouldn't describe them as interesting. Scary came a whole lot closer.

"Maybe Walters employed Joey's services as a procurer," Davinia mused. "Maybe Joey tried a little blackmail to supplement his income. Maybe the congressman decided he wasn't going to play that game."

Sam draped an arm across the back of the booth and stretched out his legs. Wedged in beside him as she was, Molly felt his hip and thigh connect with hers.

"We can 'maybe' this all night," he said slowly, "but that doesn't mitigate the fact that Walters has an alibi for the night of the murder."

"An alibi backed up by two-thousand-or-so assorted individuals," Molly muttered, stabbing at her drink.

"Hey, this is Vegas," her boss tossed out. "Two thousand people see Elvis reincarnated every night on stage at the Riviera. Thousands more watch white tigers disappear in a puff of smoke. Who's to say Walters didn't stage a theatrical appearance, then slip out when no one was looking?"

"*Quiera…*"

"Just a minute, sweetie." Patting Antonio absently on the thigh, Davinia focused her attention on the couple opposite her. "There's got to be a way to shake Walters's alibi."

"Assuming he's the killer."

"He is," Molly stated, sending Sam a glare.

Davinia tapped a nail on the table. Antonio started to speak once more, but she beat him to it.

"What we need to do is shake the man up, get him to..."

"What we need to do is let Kaplan handle this," Sam interrupted, making no effort to hide his scowl. "Josh Walters is too smart to let himself be shaken out of anything."

"*Quiera...*"

Shushing the hulking Spaniard with a wave of one hand, Davinia pounced on Sam's reply.

"Wrong! He made a big mistake when he called that lieutenant. What if she'd gotten him on tape? If he starts hearing rumors that he's under investigation and gets rattled, he may very well make another."

"I don't see it," Sam said stubbornly, shaking his head.

"He threatened this lieutenant, or so she claims. He might call Molly and try to intimidate her, too."

Or he may decide to pay her another visit, she thought with a shudder. She had no proof the same person she'd heard on the phone had slipped into her house the next night. Only her intuition, which, unfortunately, was working overtime at the moment.

"He doesn't have to call me," she said glumly. "He's got two-thousand-plus witnesses who can swear to his whereabouts at the time of the murder."

The patient Spaniard finally thrust himself into the conversation. "This *politico,* he is well known here, no? Like the movie star?"

"Very like the movie star," Davinia replied absently.

Antonio caught her chin and snared her attention

by the simple expedient of tugging her face around to him.

"Listen to me, *quiera*. Someone who does Elvis, why could he not also do this Joshua Walters?"

"Huh?"

Grinning at her less than incisive reply, he dropped a kiss on her nose. "I have been to these shows on the Strip. I have seen the Elvis and the Julio Iglesias and the Marilyn Monroe. Why could someone who does the so-talented, so-handsome Julio not also impre...impro..."

"Impersonate Joshua Walters," Davinia finished for him in awe. "Ho-ly crappoli, you just might have something there!"

Her jaw sagging, Molly stared at her boss and the brawny masseur. She couldn't quite believe what she was hearing, or that Antonio's bizarre idea actually made sense. What had happened to the nice, serene world she'd created for herself here in Vegas? It was now populated by murdered pimps. Cold-blooded killers. Maybe even a professional impersonator who stood up for a U.S. congressman at a campaign fund-raising gala attended by half of Nevada!

That was insane.

But then...

Sanity had slipped away from her the night she made that blasted phone call. No, she corrected with an accusing glare at the man beside her, it had started slipping away the day Sam moved in next door.

If he caught her look, he ignored it. Like Davinia,

he was staring at Antonio. Doubt, incredulity, and, finally, outright amusement chased across his face.

"I'd say that's as good a theory as any," he told the other man.

Antonio smugly crunched down on a nacho. Davinia grinned and flashed Molly a look of pure, feminine delight.

"Brains and brawn, girl, brains and brawn. How in the world did we get so lucky?"

By the time Molly and Sam parted from the others, her head whirled with the effects of two potent margaritas, the theories Davinia had tossed out with ruthless enthusiasm, and the press of Sam's hard, muscled thigh against hers in the narrow booth.

She walked into the night beside Sam, trying to decide which bothered her more...her body's clamoring insistence that she forget about slowing things down between them or his insistence that they stay out of the murder investigation and let Kaplan handle it.

Unlocking the Trans Am, she slid onto its leather seat. The trapped heat only added to her unsettled, disgruntled feeling. She missed the pull of the wind in her hair as she drove home through the gathering twilight, the Blazer's lights reflected in her rearview mirror. She'd put the top up this morning for the first time in ages. She'd even taken to locking her car doors.

As it had in the restaurant, a surge of resentment swept through Molly. Balling her fist, she pounded the steering wheel. Dammit, she'd come to Nevada to regain control of her life. She'd taken such joy in owning her first home, in wandering through the empty rooms and visualizing how she'd fill them. Now she'd barricaded herself behind a security system that could keep Fort Knox impregnable. She jumped at every shadow. She'd even gotten nervous about leaving the convertible's top down.

To heck with it! She was tired of sitting back and…and waiting. She wanted to *do* something.

Pulling into the garage, Molly grabbed her purse, slid out of the car, and hit the remote. A quick duck under the rumbling door brought her out into the cooling twilight. She waited while Sam tucked the Blazer into its berth next to his Mustang.

"Do you still have the tape you made last night?"

The Blazer's door thudded shut. "Yes."

"I'd like to take another look at it."

A frown settled in his gray eyes again as he ushered her inside. The house echoed only unbroken stillness. Tonight, the gleaming steel gym that took up most of his great room stood silent. No black weights rattled and clanged. No lonely lament wailed from the radio. Sam wasn't suffering tonight, thank goodness, even if he retrieved the cassette from the VCR and moved toward her with a slash between his dark brows. He tapped the videocassette against his palm.

"You sure you want to watch this again, Molly?"

"I'm sure."

"Why?"

She spun away, fighting a new surge of irritation. She didn't like having to explain herself, particularly when she knew Sam wouldn't agree with what she wanted to do. For an uncomfortable moment, she felt as though she were back in Boston again. Scowling at the jungle of smooth steel bars and beams that blocked her way, she took a deep breath and turned back to Sam.

"There was a trailer at the end of the ad. It listed dates and locations for a series of public forums Walters is attending to meet with his constituency."

"I saw it."

"I'm going to go to one of those sessions. Maybe if he sees me or hears my name, he'll know that I've recognized him and…"

"It's too risky," he said flatly. "I won't let you expose yourself to that kind of danger."

Her chin snapped up. "I don't recall asking for your permission."

Cursing his blunder, Sam knew he had to act fast if he wanted to recover. He tossed aside the cassette and moved to the gym. His hands folded around the well-worn grips of the crossbar.

"Bad word choice, Mol. Of course you don't need my permission, but I hope you'll take my advice. Let Kaplan handle this."

Let me protect you.

The words hammered in Sam's chest, worked their way to his throat. She wasn't ready to hear them, though. Anger stained her cheeks and sparked in her eyes. Struggling to keep his protective instincts on a short leash, he tried a different tact.

"You don't know Walters."

Sam could see at once that he'd pushed the wrong button.

"And you do?" Her eyes flashed green fire. "I know it's hard for you to believe that your sainted Josh Walters could kill someone in cold blood...."

"Dammit, you've convinced me, Molly. That's why it's pure idiocy for you to waltz into one of those forums and confront the man."

Without meaning to, he crowded her back until her calves hit the narrow leather bench. Or maybe he'd meant to crowd her. Hell, at this point, Sam wasn't sure of anything except a fierce headache was starting to pound in his temples, only this one had Molly Duncan's name written all over it.

"Look," she began coolly, "I'm not some lieutenant under your command, and I don't respond well to orders cloaked as advice. I appreciate your concern, but..."

"Concern, hell!"

Sam had passed concern the moment she blasted through her damned hedge and tumbled into his arms. He'd passed lust, too, although he didn't quite know when. At this particular moment, he hovered somewhere between irritation and love, which scared the hell out of him. His savage thoughts must have shown in his face. Her eyes narrowing, she issued a warning.

"I think you'd better back off, Henderson."

It was too late for that. It was probably too late the first time she flaked all over him.

"Not this time, Duncan."

"Excuse me?"

"I backed off last night. I'm not retreating again."

"Oh?"

She folded her arms across her chest. Against the superstructure of polished steel, she was all bronze knit and angry female.

"You're treading shaky ground here, Major. Real shaky."

"I got that impression," he drawled.

"Let's get something straight. I left Boston to get away from a man who tried to dictate my choices. I don't want or need another one trying the same thing here in Vegas."

The idea that she would lump him in the same category as the wimp who let her walk out of his life without a backward glance rubbed Sam exactly the wrong way.

"So what are you going to do if I press you too hard or too soon, sweetheart? Run away again?"

The soft taunt cut through the air between them, as alive and explosive as electricity.

Molly sucked in a swift breath. He wasn't talking about Walters now, or her determination to attend one of the congressman's forums. With a seismic movement she'd somehow missed, the ground had suddenly shifted.

This was between her and Sam. About her and Sam. Despite his gruff refusal to back off, he wouldn't force her. Molly knew that, as surely as she sensed that he'd tumble her down onto the leather bench behind her if she so much as blinked.

Still simmering, she tilted her head back. His tanned skin stretched across his cheekbones. The edge of his jaw could have cut glass. But it wasn't pain that darkened his eyes, she saw with a lurch. It was hunger, raw and primitive, and a fierceness that skidded right past lust into an emotion that made Molly's heart trip.

Her anger fractured, breaking into smaller shards that splintered away. In its place came an answering emotion so strong that she didn't try to fight it anymore.

"No, Sam," she said at last. "I'm not running away. This time I'm standing my ground."

Chapter 11

Molly didn't remain standing for long.

At her soft declaration, Sam's eyes flared with a satisfaction that looked possessive and felt primal. He moved a step closer, still gripping the crossbar, the muscles in his arms bunching.

Molly felt caged by the steel around her. Claimed by the man before her. Trapped in a way that should have panicked her, but didn't. Much. He must have sensed her brief flutter of uncertainty. His voice dropped to a rough cured leather.

"If it makes you feel any better about what's about to happen between us, you can have my couch. I don't use it, anyway."

Her hands trembled with the need to slide them up, over those wide shoulders, around his neck.

"What do you use, Sam?"

He smiled, a slow slash of male amusement that had Molly's nails digging into her palms.

"Upstairs, I use the bed. Downstairs, the easy chair in the corner. The floor. The..."

"Okay, okay, I get the picture."

She drew in a shaky breath. He was so close. Too close. She could feel his heat. See the tendon that corded in his neck like rawhide thongs. She made one last stand before surrendering completely to the desire that raced through her like summer wildfire.

"Just remember that I don't take orders very well, Major."

"I'll keep that in mind."

"No military dictatorships or heavy-handed tactics allowed on either side."

"Got it. Anything else?"

"Not..." Molly dragged her tongue across dry lips. "Not that I can think of."

Who was she kidding? With Sam's mouth only inches from her own, she could barely breathe. Thinking had passed into the realm of the impossible.

"Good."

His knee nudged hers apart, separating them. He edged her backward, until she straddled the narrow, padded bench. Her skirt inched up her thighs with a soft slither. Her breath hitched somewhere in the middle of her throat.

"Why do I get the feeling we're not going to make it upstairs?"

"Molly, sweetheart, you're not going to make it to the floor."

The husky promise sent her stomach into a roll. She stared up at Sam's eyes, unsure where this searing urgency between them was going but in more of a hurry to get there with each passing second.

"Why don't you put your hands over mine?" he suggested in the same, low rumble.

Trembling with anticipation, Molly uncurled her fists and laid her palms over the backs of his hands where they gripped the bar.

"Now lift."

She pulled herself up, just enough for his thighs to slide under hers. Her skirt bunched at her hips. The zipper of his jeans rubbed against her panties.

And still he didn't touch her! They were thigh to thigh, breath to breath, and he didn't let go of the damned crossbar.

It only took one flex of Sam's biceps for Molly to understand why. He pulled downward. The steel cables behind her rattled. The weights clanked upward. The bar lowered, and Molly came down with it. Spread wide now, she pressed even more intimately against the ridge that had formed under Sam's jeans.

He kept her there, straddling his hips, until she turned liquid. Then slowly, so slowly, he let the bar…and Molly…rise. The exquisite, erotic pressure eased. Before she'd steadied her senses, he brought her down again.

Then again.

And again.

"Sam!" she gasped as the molten fire spread from

her belly to her breasts to her brain. "We need to…shed some clothes…before I explode."

"No, we don't."

The rough edge to his voice rasped like a file on her jagged senses. That, and the way Sam slid one hand free of hers to unsnap his jeans. She barely heard the sound of his zipper over the thundering of her pulse. Her skin jumped when he tugged her panties sideways across her wet, slick flesh.

Flexing his thighs, he positioned himself under her. Molly slid slowly onto his rigid shaft. The sense of joining was so profound, so complete, that she decided then and there not to waste her money on unnecessary furniture. Instead, she'd invest in a Universal gym for every room of her house. His house. Whichever house they happened to occupy at the moment.

Slowly, Sam pulled her into a seductive rhythm. Down, up, down. The weights rattled. The cables whirred. The leather bench slicked under their hips. Too soon, Molly felt herself start to spin, higher and tighter.

When Sam's thighs flexed under her, she knew she was close to the edge. She couldn't stand the thought of going over without touching him, without tasting him. Abandoning the crossbar, she fumbled with the buttons on his cotton shirt. Three gave. Two popped loose under her frantic hands. When she bared as much of him as she could manage, Molly wrapped her arms around his neck and her legs around his waist.

When her climax came rushing upward, she did a little flexing of her own. Her muscles clenched with a skill that surprised her and wrung a groan out of Sam. He splayed his hands on her hips, driving her down, down. His body thrust up, taking her with it.

She let out a sound somewhere between a sob and a screech. Light and dark together in a kaleidoscope of pure, pulsing pleasure.

Molly drifted back into awareness sometime later. She wasn't sure exactly when she and Sam had abandoned the hard, narrow bench for the hard, flat floor. Or when they'd jettisoned most of their outer clothes. She *was* sure that she'd never, ever, experienced such bone-melting, soul-shattering union.

She propped herself up on one elbow, drinking in the sight of the man sprawled beside her. He looked like some big mountain cat lazing in the sun, those lethal muscles slack under his sleek, tanned hide. His dark hair stood in short spikes. His right shoulder carried two little red crescents where her fingernails had unintentionally gone too deep.

She bent over and touched her mouth to the marks. He grunted, an indistinguishable male sound that could have been an invitation to continue or a warning that he hadn't recovered full consciousness yet. Molly smiled and decided to test the waters.

"About that couch...?"

"It's yours," he muttered, not opening his eyes.

"Why don't we...?"

She hesitated. She'd never propositioned a man

before, much less a man as complex, as aggravating, as intoxicating as Sam Henderson. One of his lids squinched open. Through the screen of his lashes, he squinted up at her.

''Why don't we what, Mol?''

She could do this. She could take the next step. She could tell him that she wanted him in her life. In her bed. In her heart.

''Why don't we share it? The couch, I mean.''

''You sure?''

''Yes. Well...'' Her fingertip traced a dark swirl. ''Yes.''

''Okay.''

With that, he closed his eye again and gave every appearance of a man whose only concern at that moment was catching a few z's.

Molly's hand stilled. Her ridiculously thumping heart gave a small thud.

That was it? She'd just suggested that they take up joint occupancy for some unspecified period in the near future, and all he had to offer in reply was a single, laconic 'okay'?

Well, what had she expected? A rapture of delight? A passionate declaration of undying love? She hadn't exactly gushed over the idea, either. And, a nagging little voice reminded her, she'd been the one to pull back before, to suggest they take this slow.

Contrarily, she now wanted Sam to press her for a more definite commitment. Or at least show some signs of wanting one. She sat up, giving the curl of dark hair wrapped around her finger an annoyed tweak in the process. That, at least, got both his eyes open.

"Ouch!"

"Sorry," she muttered, groping for the puddle of bronze knit that was her dress. "If you can stay awake long enough to turn on the VCR, I want to watch that video."

"Right. The video."

Sam dragged on his jeans, fighting the resistance that caught at him with the force of a tail hook hitting the arresting barrier. He didn't want to watch the damned tape. More to the point, he didn't want Molly to watch it and follow through with her hare-brained scheme of confronting a possible killer.

He'd learned his lesson, though. She'd warned him in her blunt, inimitable style that she didn't respond well to a firm hand on the reins. Hell, to *any* hand on the reins. She'd offered to share an as-yet-undefined part of her life with him in the form of his leather sofa. Sam wasn't going to jeopardize that hesitant offer by pointing out again the idiocy of what she planned to do.

He didn't have to like it, though.

He liked it even less when the color faded from Molly's face as Josh Walters's smooth, cultured voice rolled across the room.

"...the welfare reform bill I introduced last year does guarantee every person's right to a job."

The scene faded. An American flag fluttered. The announcer came on, and a trailer appeared at the bottom of the screen announcing the congressman's up-coming public appearances.

"UNLV," Molly muttered as the printed message flashed by. "Thursday, September eleventh. That's tonight!"

They'd missed that opportunity, Sam thought with grim satisfaction.

Her eyes narrowed on the scrolling words. "Saturday, the thirteenth, at the Nellis Officers' Club, 8:00 p.m. Tuesday, the sixteenth, at the Cashman Field Center, right before the baseball game...."

She'd seen enough. Spinning around, she pinned Sam with a look that challenged him far more than the mild question that came with it.

"Can I get onto the base without a military ID?"

The cops at the front gate could issue her a pass, but they both knew she wouldn't need one. She wasn't going anywhere without him. Sam conceded with something less than grace.

"My car has a sticker," he said gruffly. "I'll drive. I'll also call out to the base tomorrow and find out whether the appearance is purely political or in conjunction with some official function. You," he instructed, trying not to let it sound too much like an order, "had better call Kaplan and advise him what we're doing."

Molly hugged that "we" to her chest as Sam scooped her up and hugged *her* to his chest. Disagreement was stamped all over his strong, rugged features, but he'd passed the test.

* * *

By unspoken agreement, Molly spent the rest of Thursday night in Sam's bed. She then spent most of Friday morning avoiding Davinia's smug glances and unsubtle questions about when she and Sam intended to tear down the oleander hedge and merge their properties.

"We haven't gotten to any discussion of merging yet," Molly finally informed her persistent boss. "We're only at the your-place-or-mine? stage."

Davinia dropped into the chair in front of Molly's desk, kicked off her three-inch heels, and crossed her ankles on top of the desk with a slither of expensive stockings.

"Honey, I'm working on husband number four. You keep moving at this pace and you might not bag number one before you're forty."

"For heaven's sake, I've only known Sam for a little more than a week. Well, I've known him for longer than that, I suppose but only *known* him for…" She threw up her hands. "Okay, okay, I've known him long enough to recognize that he's special."

"Special." Her boss rolled her eyes. "He's trophy quality, Mol. And I'm not just referring to those awesome abs or preposterous pecs. If it were me, I'd already have him stuffed and mounted."

"I'm sure you would. I'm not the great white hunter you are, though. After my last, disastrous fling with love, I'm taking things more slowly."

"More slowly?" Davinia huffed in derision. "You're moving at the speed of road kill."

"Besides," Molly added, ignoring the gibe, "Sam

has a few issues of his own to work through before he lets himself get, uh, stuffed.''

The older woman cocked her head. Her shining, blunt-cut platinum hair feathered across one shoulder. "Like what?"

"Like a tendency to issue orders, for one thing."

"And?"

She hesitated, knowing how closemouthed Sam was about his injury but needing to share her own, growing worry for him.

"And a pain that keeps him awake and prowling all night sometimes."

Her boss's feet slid off the desk and hit the floor with a well-mannered thump. Genuine concern filled her turquoise eyes. "What kind of pain?"

Briefly, Molly recounted the few details Sam had told her of his accident.

"He shrugs off any discussion of his headaches, but he did tell me that he has to meet another medical evaluation board in a few months. I didn't understand all the Air Force jargon. All I know is that he's on some kind of a temporary retirement or suspension list. If his condition doesn't improve, this medical board will put him out to pasture permanently."

Davinia's legal antennae snapped to attention. "He can fight a permanent discharge. He's not completely incapacitated. If he can't fly, he can certainly serve in some other capacity."

Molly shook her head. "I don't think he'll do that."

She'd gained enough insight into Sam Henderson

in the past week to know he wouldn't put himself back in uniform when those blinding headaches could hit him at any moment.

"Tell him to call me," her boss suggested briskly. "I know an attorney who specializes in worker's comp and on-the-job injury cases. He might know something about the military system. If he doesn't, I'm sure he can find someone who does."

Molly felt a rush of warm gratitude, remembering how only a few days ago Davinia had offered to involve her ex-husband in a lawsuit on her behalf against her pesky neighbor. Now she was ready to take up that same, pesky neighbor's cause. Her boss was nothing if not generous-hearted.

"Thanks, I'll tell him."

Davinia got up to leave a few moments later. Sighing, she reported that she was having lunch with Antonio at the health food eatery in the spa where he worked.

"Can you believe it, he's actually got me enjoying bean sprouts?"

Molly could believe it. From the droll expression on her boss's face, she guessed it wouldn't be long until Davinia had the handsome Spaniard stuffed and mounted. Mounted, anyway.

Smiling, she reached for the phone. She'd promised Sam she'd call Detective Kaplan and tell him about Walters's appearance at the Nellis Officers' Club tomorrow night. Might as well get it over with. He'd probably raise the same objections Sam had to Molly's planned expedition.

To her surprise, he didn't. When he called back some hours later, he turned the idea over, examining it from all angles.

"It might work," he said at last. "We'll wire you. If you startle any kind of a reaction out of him, we can move in. What time is this big event?"

"Eight o'clock. Sam called this morning to make sure."

"What kind of function is it?"

"It's a formal banquet in honor of the Air Force's anniversary. Walters is the guest speaker. Supposedly, he's going to use the occasion to unveil the second of his three new strategies for protecting jobs and growing industry in his district, which includes the base."

"Tell you what. I'll bring one of our specialists by your place before you leave for this banquet tomorrow to fit you with the wire, then we'll go to this party with you."

"All right."

"Since we'll be on federal property, I'll have to coordinate my presence with the base. The top cop out there's a pretty cool head. He'll give us whatever backup we need...if we need it."

The grim possibility gave Molly pause. Suddenly, the prospect of going face-to-face with Walters didn't hold quite the same appeal it had before. She hung up a few moments later, alternating between a guilty regret at having started down this road and a determination not to chicken out.

* * *

As she'd anticipated, Sam didn't like the idea of Kaplan outfitting Molly with a wire any more than he liked the idea of her confronting Walters. She told him about it later that evening over a candlelit patio dinner of chicken and mushroom crepes, compliments of a French restaurant she'd stopped at on the way home. The bottle of light, fragrant pinot blanc came compliments of Sam's well-stocked assortment of California wine.

Sam, she noticed, had barely touched either the crepes or the wine. The flickering candlelight didn't disguise the lines bracketing his mouth. Nor did Buck Randall's soft lament, which Molly had suggested for background music when she'd taken in Sam's rigid shoulders.

"Kaplan is as crazy as you and your boss if he thinks someone like Josh Walters is going to say anything incriminating in public."

"He's reaching, Sam, just as you and Antonio were last night when you tossed around that impersonator bit."

"That's a lot more plausible than having you waltz into the club and spook Walters into a confession."

"I suggested the possibility of an impersonator standing in for Walters to Kaplan. He's going to nose around, see if any of the actors on the Strip know of an act like that."

"Oh, great." Sam's fork clattered onto his plate. "If Walters didn't know that he's under suspicion before, he soon will. Why not just post a notice on the marquee in front of Caesars?"

They both knew the detective would handle the inquiries discreetly. Molly didn't try to argue the point, however. Her heart ached for the man across the table. Like the fabled character in Robert Louis Stevenson's novel, Sam's darker side was in ascendancy. Unlike Dr. Jekyll, though, he wouldn't let the Mr. Hyde side of his personality win control of his being. He'd fight the stabbing pain with everything he had in him.

Searching desperately for a way to help him with the continuing battle, Molly steered the conversation away from the contentious issue of tomorrow night into less provocative channels.

"Speaking of my crazy boss, Davinia mentioned that she has a friend...an attorney...who specializes in claims for on-the-job injuries. She offered to get in touch with him for you if you want representation when you go before this medical board you told me about."

Sam tipped his head back, studying her through narrowed eyes.

"Tell her thanks, but no thanks. I'm not going to fight the board's final decision, Molly."

"I didn't think you would," she replied calmly. "So what *are* you going to do, Sam? Besides make love to me two or three times a day, every day, until we wear each other or the leather on the bench out completely?"

Her nonchalance startled a surprised look out of him. Slowly, almost imperceptibly, he relaxed.

"I've had a few offers. Kicked around a few ideas."

Curious, she swirled the pale liquid in her glass. "Like what?"

"Like starting my own computer-based search service for classic car parts, for one."

Molly stared at him over the rim of her wineglass, surprised and impressed. She hadn't connected the sophisticated array of computer equipment she'd glimpsed in Sam's upstairs study with his all-consuming passion for old cars.

"Sounds like a fascinating hobby."

"I wasn't thinking in terms of a hobby, sweetheart. Classic cars are big business. Avid restorers pay thousands of dollars for original parts."

"You're kidding!"

"No, ma'am. The finders fees alone would keep you in pinot blanc for the rest of your life...or in enough beer to eradicate every freckle on your long, luscious body."

"I don't have freckles anywhere but on my nose," she informed him loftily.

A wicked grin tugged at his mouth. "Shows what you know."

Molly caught her breath as he eased his chair back.

"Why don't you bring your wine inside?" he suggested. "You can finish it while I work out. Then...maybe...we can work out together."

Matching her grin to his, she picked up her glass. "Sounds good to me."

Chapter 12

Molly pirouetted slowly in front of the bathroom mirror, studying her image doubtfully.

Was her black dress too much? Or not enough?

Sam had told her that the military would wear their uniforms to the banquet tonight. The civilian men would be in tuxes, and the women would pull out all the stops. With that somewhat nebulous guidance, Molly had debated between her only long gown, a floor-length slide of shimmering gold lamé, and this above-the-knee cocktail dress. The lamé was more formal, but this little number had grabbed her heart and a good chunk of her bank account when she'd spotted it in Saks at Fashion Show Mall. She'd cheerfully delayed her planned furniture purchases for another month in order to possess it.

There wasn't much to it, though, on top or on bottom. Sequined strips of black satin banded her breasts and the mid-thigh hem, without a great deal of black crepe in between. Oh, well, the sinful creation certainly pulled out every stop she had.

Clipping on a pair of square rhinestone-and-jet earrings, Molly gave her upswept hair a final pat, then picked up her black mesh evening bag and headed downstairs. At the sound of her stiletto heels on the oak steps, Sam pushed himself out of the single rattan chair in her living room.

When she caught sight of him standing straight and tall at the bottom of the stairs, she stopped abruptly.

"Wow!"

If her little black dress constituted close to the minimum coverage required by law, just the opposite held true for Sam. What seemed like a half acre of midnight blue uniform molded his broad shoulders and otherwise mouthwatering form. The short, tailored jacket sported silver-edged shoulder boards embroidered with gold oak leaves, shiny silver wings and an array of colorful medals. A snowy white pleated shirt formed a startling contrast. The navy satin bow tie and cummerbund circling his lean waist matched the stripe running down the outsides of his pants' legs. With his neatly trimmed dark hair, gray eyes and tanned skin, he looked like every woman's fantasy come to life…in or out of uniform.

"I'll see that wow and raise you one," Sam murmured, devouring her from neck to knees.

The sudden heat in his eyes sent a prickle of pleasure through Molly. He'd seen her at her worst, with brown mush layered across her cheeks and coffee staining her front. Now he was seeing her at her best, and he certainly seemed to appreciate the view. For a moment she could have sworn she was Cinderella, about to depart for the ball with her handsome prince.

Then a small frown puckered Sam's brow. "I thought you said Kaplan was coming here to wire you?"

Molly slid back into reality with a thud.

"He is." She twisted the gold bracelet watch on her left wrist to check the time. "He said he'd be here by seven. I wonder where he is?"

"I'm wondering where he's going to plant his listening device."

"Right here," she replied dryly, dangling her little bag by one hand. "I'm not letting this sucker out of my hands for the rest of the night."

"Just so you know, I have the same plans for you." He strolled forward and curled a knuckle to brush it down her cheek. "It's not too late to change your mind about this, Molly."

For a moment, she was tempted. Really tempted. Confronting Congressman Walters in a public forum had seemed like a good idea when she'd first thought about it. Now, with the face-off imminent, she wasn't ashamed to admit she was having second and third thoughts.

If the bell hadn't rung at that moment, she might even have wimped out and saved both herself and

Sam the terror that followed. Instead, she merely
smiled.

"We're all dressed up. We might as well go to
the ball."

Detective Kaplan had dressed for the ball, too.
Dark-jowled, dark-eyed and obviously uncomfortable in a tux that strained over his stomach, he
greeted both her and Sam, then introduced Detective
Sergeant Dee Santos. The short, henna-haired Hispanic, looking more elegant than her partner in pale,
oyster-colored satin pants and a matching jacket,
skimmed a quick look over Molly's outfit.

"Nice threads."

"Thanks."

"I hope I don't have to try to conceal anything
under them."

Pointedly avoiding Sam's sardonic look, Molly
held out the black mesh evening bag.

"Will this work?"

"Perfectly!"

Propping her briefcase on the gnarled cypress tree
stump that did duty as an end table, Santos snapped
open the lid. The bite-sized package of electronics
she pulled out looked more like a handheld tape recorder than the high-tech bit of electronics Kaplan
had described to Molly. The police officer fiddled
with a couple of protruding wires, adjusted an an-
tenna, and flicked a switch. Static screeched through
the air, then the tiny black box lapsed into silence.

"This little baby will pick up normal conversation
with no problem," Santos said as she clipped the

black button inside the lining of the purse. "We'll have a lot of background noise to filter out at the club, though. It'll help if you get as up close and personal with the target as possible."

Target. Molly's skin rippled at the word.

Folding over the mesh flap, Santos handed her back the bag. "Better yet, try to get our boy alone, off to a corner or in one of the anterooms."

"No way," Sam said flatly.

Both detectives looked at him in surprise.

"I don't think that's a good idea," he said with a little less whip. "First, we're dealing with a man suspected of murder here. Second, it's going to look odd, to say the least, if I stand around twiddling my thumbs while another man whisks my woman off to a corner or a private room to huddle."

His blatant use of the possessive caught Molly off guard. Sam, too, if the quick, frowning glance he threw her was any indication. Her independent spirit instantly raised its head, but her objection formed with something less than its usual force. Molly didn't have any great desire to huddle in a corner with Congressman Walters. Even more to the point, a contrary, deeply visceral part of her wanted Sam to claim her, to tell her he was ready to share more than his couch with her.

"I suppose you have a point there," Dee Santos conceded with a shrug. "We'll just have to hope the receiver filters out the background noise enough to keep any conversation between Ms. Duncan and the congressman audible." Flicking the switch once more, she nodded to Molly. "Say something. Anything. I need a voice print."

"A voice print?" Interest flared in Molly's eyes. "Does this device record individual vocal signatures?"

"Not signatures, exactly. The technology isn't that advanced yet. The best we can do is run a print that helps distinguish between speakers when there's a lot of background noise, as there will be tonight." She glanced down at the palm-sized device she held in her hand. "Okay, I've got you. Ready to go?"

Swiping a damp palm down the side of her dress, Molly nodded. Kaplan caught the small movement. His jowls creased in a reassuring smile.

"Don't worry, Ms. Duncan. Detective Santos and I are meeting the base chief of security at the club. We'll have you covered from the moment you walk in the front door."

"So will I," Sam said grimly as he followed Molly and the others to the front door.

Molly had only visited a military post once before. Nellis Air Force Base, she soon discovered, bore little resemblance to ramshackle, WWII-era Fort Devans a few miles outside of Boston. Even in the descending darkness, she noted the professionalism of the guard who saluted and waved them through the gate. As they followed the stream of traffic heading for the Officers' Club, a jet roared down the runway, its engines glowing like twin red suns as it soared into the night. Another followed a few seconds later, adding to the thunder that rolled across the sky.

The military honor guard that snapped to attention and whipped their swords into a flashing arch at the entrance to the Officers' Club impressed her even more. Spit-shined and sharp in their white ascots and blue uniforms, the men and women who formed the honor guard looked young and invincible and proud.

Sam returned their salute, greeting several by name as he escorted Molly up the steps. A square-jawed young sergeant opened the door for them.

"Good to see you back, Major Henderson."

"Good to be back, Brent," Sam answered easily. "I heard that AGS aced the ORI last month. You must have been TDY at the time."

Molly had no idea what the alphabet soup of acronyms meant, but the huge grin that split the young man's face told her it was some kind of inside joke. Taking a moment to simply absorb the unfamiliar sights and sounds, she waited beside a bank of feathery ferns while Sam stepped up to a linen-draped table to confirm the last-minute table reservations he'd wrangled for them.

He was just turning back to Molly when a husky voice floated through the crowded hall.

"Sam? I thought that was you."

A tall, sloe-eyed woman with a sweep of rich auburn hair strolled forward. The side slit in her floor-length uniform skirt showed just enough leg for several men to turn for a second look.

Molly had never seen the stunning officer before,

but the husky, dark-as-chocolate voice struck a chord. Memory kicked in when the woman flowed into Sam's arms with a naturalness that said she'd been there before.

This had to be the woman who'd answered Sam's phone the first time Molly called to complain about his music. The one who promised to give him the message when he got out of the shower.

Sam hadn't gotten the message. Observing the expression on the officer's face as she practically fused with Sam in the crowded hallway, Molly wasn't surprised. Obviously, she'd had other things on her mind that night.

Tonight, too.

"You're looking great," she told him. "Better than great. Good enough to eat."

Laughing, Sam disengaged. "You're looking pretty good, too, Janet. How's the intelligence business?"

The redhead wrinkled her nose. "Not very intelligent. We're going through another manpower reduction, just when things are heating up in the Gulf again."

She angled her head, her eyes unreadable, but Molly's keen ear didn't miss the intimate concern that rippled through her voice.

"How are you feeling?"

Lifting his head, Sam met Molly's interested gaze. "Better than I have in a long time," he replied with a slow, private smile. "Come on, I want you to meet someone."

In the few seconds it took for Sam to escort the officer across the hallway, the two women communicated with swift, unerring accuracy. Molly had no difficulty interpreting or answering the silent message that flashed in the slanted, violet eyes.

He was mine first.

Tough. He's mine now.

This time, her independent spirit didn't so much as whisper a protest at the flagrant use of the possessive.

"Captain Green and I have already met," she said when Sam had performed the introductions. "Or rather, we've spoken."

"Have we?"

"I think you answered the phone one night when I called Sam's house to talk to him about Buck Randall."

The redhead's nose wrinkled once again. Obviously, she didn't remember the irate phone message she'd promised to pass on.

"Are you a fan, too?"

"I don't know if I'd go quite that far. Let's just say Sam's encouraging me to develop more of an appreciation for the man's artistry."

Once again, the two women communicated without words. Something that might have been regret shone in the captain's extraordinary eyes for a moment, then her mouth curved in her first genuine smile.

"Better you than me. Good luck."

"Thanks."

She turned to the man at her side. "I'm here with Doc and Mindy and her husband. Would you two like to join us? We can do some quick table shuffling."

"Maybe we'll join you for a drink after dinner," Sam said easily. "We're sitting at one of the 442d tables."

"Uh, oh! You're in for a lively night, Molly. The 442d holds the record for the most trips to the grog bowl. See you later."

"That sounds ominous."

Sam grinned and edged her aside to let another group of officers and their ladies pass.

"Don't worry. They don't go after civilians... much. There are Kaplan and Santos."

With reinforcements, Molly noted. A balding, ramrod straight officer with a glittering array of medals on his chest accompanied the two detectives.

"Good to see you, Sam," he said, thrusting out his hand.

"You, too, sir."

"How's the head?"

"Still there. This is Ms. Duncan. Molly Duncan. Molly, this is Colonel Scott, chief of security for the base."

Flinty blue eyes measured her. Evidently she passed his test. His craggy face creased into a smile.

"Why don't we go into the club manager's office?" he suggested. "We can go over the security arrangements there and test this equipment you're wearing?"

"Carrying," Sam amended dryly.

The colonel had more sense than to comment on that one.

Fifteen minutes later, Molly and Sam joined the throng slowly filling the club's main ballroom and made their way to their table. They halted frequently while Sam returned greetings and introduced Molly to a host of friends and acquaintances. Halfway across the room, she gave up trying to remember names and faces. There were too many.

Her nerves fluttered even more than the blue-and-silver foil streamers draped from the chandeliers to form a glittering overhead canopy. Hundreds of long, slender blue tapers flickered in glass hurricane lamps. The flickering light added to the festive air, but made it impossible to see much more than a few yards away.

She clutched Sam's arm, skimming the sea of midnight blue that surrounded her. The few civilians in tuxes scattered through the crowd almost got lost amid the colorful glitter of medals and glinting silver shoulder boards.

Almost.

A few stood out. Several of them Molly recognized instantly. One was the mayor of Las Vegas, a portly, red-faced man already sweating profusely. Another was a real estate developer who chaired the Chamber of Commerce, which met regularly with the Tourist Bureau. But it was the tall, distinguished civilian with the shock of prematurely gray hair who riveted her attention. Her fingers dug into Sam's arm as he pulled out her chair.

"There he is," she hissed in his ear.

"I saw him."

"Shouldn't we go over and talk to him?"

"Not now," he said calmly. "Mr. Vice is about to ring the chimes. We'll have to wait until the smoking lamp is lit."

"Whenever that is," Molly muttered.

A long, lanky major with a white-walled buzz cut and an infectious grin jumped up to assist Sam with the onerous task of pushing in her chair.

"That, sweet thang, is right after the rubber chicken and right before the speeches. I'm Rock, short for Rocket, as in straight up. What in the world is a first-class hottie like you doing with Drac?"

"Drac?" Molly arched a look at Sam. "As in Dracula?"

"As in Dracm," Rock supplied, "a fourteenth-century dragon who owned the skies and belched fire, among other things. Why don't you dump the old man and run away with me?"

Startled, Molly glanced from him to the woman seated on the other side of his empty chair. The laughing mother-to-be folded her hands across her bulging stomach.

"Please! Take him off my hands and I'll give you my firstborn. My second, third, fourth and fifth, too. Heck, I'll even throw in the dog, and run off with the old man you came with as soon as I pop."

"Which we hope won't happen tonight," Sam

drawled. "You provided enough entertainment by delivering number five at the squadron picnic." Grinning, he bent over to brush a kiss across her mouth. "Hello, Peg."

"Hello, Drac."

"Got this one named yet? As best I recall, the last one went by 'it' for three months while Rock tried to sell you on 'Falcon.'"

"As a matter of fact, we have a name all picked out." Her hand reached up to curl around his. "How does Samuel Czcynsky sound to you?"

His strong, tanned fingers gripped hers. "Pretty damn good."

She clung to his hand for a moment, sharing what was obviously a vivid memory. Rock shared it with Molly a few moments later, after the flurry of introductions had been completed and Sam turned his attention to the bashful young wife seated on his other side.

"Drac and I participated in some cold weather tests a year or so ago," he told her quietly. "My plane took a bird strike and I had to bail out over some nasty seas. Drac stayed right over me, talking to me, swearing at me, threatening to wring my scrawny neck if I died on him. The rescue chopper arrived and hauled my frozen butt out of the water just before hypothermia took me under for the last time."

He paused, his face seeming to fold in on itself as an icy vision held him in its grip.

"Drac made it back to base on pure fumes, and

Peg swore she'd name this one after him whether it was a boy or girl. She thinks a lot of him." His gaze slid past Molly's shoulder to the man at her side. "We all do," he finished softly.

"So I've gathered."

"What about you?"

"Excuse me?"

"What do you think of the Drac Man?"

The seriousness in Rock's homely handsome face told Molly that she'd better give the right answer. It came easy.

"I think a lot of him, too."

"Good."

When someone else at the table claimed the young pilot's attention, Molly leaned back. A small tilt to her head allowed her to study the man with his arm looped along the back of her chair. For all the jokes and banter being tossed around, it was obvious that Sam commanded these officers' respect. Only gradually did she realize that he'd also commanded most of them in battle. Almost all of them were veterans of Desert Storm. A few had also seen some hot action in Bosnia.

Sam belonged here, she thought with an aching sense of loss...for him, for the men and women he once led. He was a warrior at heart. He and the others all shared the same values, the same dangers, the same dedication to their country. Yet as incredible as it seemed, he harbored no bitterness as a result of his accident, no resentment toward an Air Force that would soon put him permanently on the shelf.

He was, as Davinia had said, real trophy quality.

At that moment, the last of Molly's hesitations fell away. Watching his easy smile, seeing his gray eyes light with laughter, feeling the warmth of the arm that circled her bare shoulders, she felt herself sliding the rest of the way down that slippery slope Buck Randall had called love. Her heart opened, and she knew her slide wouldn't stop for a long, long time.

He turned and caught her look. His smile tipped into one of his patented, Sam-only grins. Curling his arm around her shoulders, he drew her closer and bent down to be heard over the noise of the crowd.

"You keep looking at me like that," he murmured, "and we might have to slip out to the car for a few minutes to give those bucket seats one more try."

"You keep blowing in my ear like that and it will take more than a few minutes."

He started to reply, only to be cut off by the squawk of a microphone. Molly jumped, almost hitting Sam in the chin with her head, and shot a quick look at the little black evening bag resting beside her plate. To her profound relief, the noise had come from the center of the room, where a nervous lieutenant on a dais thumped the mike in front of him, raising another squawk.

"Ladies and gentlemen, please take your seats."

A moment later, the sound of a gavel slamming down thundered through the speakers. Molly jumped again and swiveled around to face the head table. A crew-cut colonel surveyed the vast assemblage.

"The mess is called to order. Mr. Vice, you may proceed."

The ceremonies got underway immediately. The honor guard paraded the colors, an astonishing litany of toasts were drunk, Mr. Vice pointed out infractions of the mess rules, intentional or otherwise, and the president sent various miscreants to the alcoholic and nonalcoholic grog bowls placed strategically around the room.

Molly rose when the other civilian women rose, drank when the others lifted their glasses, smiled at the sometimes incomprehensible jargon and inside jokes. Through it all, however, her gaze kept straying back to the couple seated at the head table on either side of the colonel.

Congressman Joshua Walters, and his wife, Jessica MacGiver Walters. One gray and smoothly handsome. The other raven-haired and elegant in rippling silver satin. She smiled out on the crowd with a remote sort of graciousness that could only come with wealth and long years in the spotlight.

Or did that faint, smiling reserve stem from other, darker sources? Did she really know what kind of man she'd married? Could she have any idea that her husband might be a murderer?

Molly was locked so intently on the wife that a few moments passed before she realized that the husband had locked on her.

Her head snapped back. Her heart skipped.

Walters gave no sign that he recognized her. No evidence that he'd noted her reaction. His expression didn't change. His gaze didn't falter. He observed her for another instant or two, then turned his head in response to some comment from the woman at his side.

Molly clenched her hands under the tablecloth to still their trembling. Cold sweat dewed her back and bare shoulders.

What had she expected? she thought savagely. That his composure would shatter at the sight of her? If he were the killer, he knew her name, but that didn't necessarily mean he knew her face. Even if he did, he might think her presence here tonight just a coincidence.

She was still trying to think of a subtle way to let him know she hadn't arrived at the club by chance when fate, in the shape of a well-endowed young lieutenant, took the matter out of her hands.

Chapter 13

"Ladies and gentlemen, the smoking lamp is lit."

Cheers and whistles greeted Mr. Vice's announcement. Four-hundred-plus chairs scraped back. Replete males stretched out legs and recharged glasses. Brightly gowned women made a general exodus to the ladies' room.

"Would you like to go powder your nose?"

Molly smiled at the shy young captain's wife across from her. "No, thanks."

"This is your last chance before the speeches start," the pregnant Peg chimed in. "Unless that gorgeous creation you're wearing comes equipped with a relief tube, you could be in trouble."

"No relief tube," Molly replied, "but I'm pretty tough."

"I can attest to that," Sam added with a lazy grin.

''Why don't we get some fresh air instead? Bring your purse, sweetheart.''

The contrast between Sam's casual endearment and his reference to her evening bag jolted Molly. She caught his eye and with it the swift reminder of the reason they'd attended this gathering of eagles.

Her pulse quickening, she glanced past him to the head table. Jessica Walters and the General's wife had already started weaving their way through the crowd. Cigars in hands, their husbands headed for the wall of glass doors that opened onto a patio strung with white lights and silvery blue streamers.

''Fresh air sounds good,'' Molly got out, her throat tight.

Sam guided her through the crowd, his hand warm and reassuring at the small of her back. She clutched the little mesh bag to her chest and swept the ballroom with a quick, searching look. A flash of pale, oyster-colored satin caught her eye. At a table tucked in a distant corner, Dee Santos nodded imperceptibly. Her shoulder-length sweep of hennaed hair hid all sign of the wire that ran from her earpiece to the recorder in her jacket pocket. Molly didn't see Kaplan or the ramrod straight Colonel Scott amid the forest of men in dark uniforms, but she knew they were somewhere in the vicinity.

The glass patio doors slid open on smooth, silent bearings. A desert breeze, warm after the air-conditioned chill of the huge ballroom, brushed Molly's skin. Glass chinked against glass as bartenders poured drinks at the two small bars set up at either end of the patio. The haunting strains of "Wind Beneath My Wings" drifted through speakers. A few couples swayed to the music, pressed close together by the intimacy of the minuscule, open-air dance floor.

The setting should have been magical. A blending of elegance and pride, of romance and seduction. On any other night, Molly would have melted into Sam's arms and let the sheer beauty of the moment carry her away. Tonight, she absorbed the ambiance through the filter of wire-tight nerves. Her whole being was focused on the man who stood only a few yards away, surrounded by a small clutch of men and women.

Josh Walters was in his element. Urbane, confident, relaxed, he smiled and held court with practiced ease. He hadn't given his speech yet. During introductions of the head table, he and his wife had merely stood and waved in acknowledgment of the warm round of applause they received. Yet Molly could hear his voice in her head. Every well-modulated syllable echoed with the clarity of a bell, punctuated by Joey Bennett's terrified pleas and the splat of gunfire.

With seeming casualness, Sam guided her across the patio. The small crowd around the congressman eddied and flowed. Two couples moved away, heading back to the ballroom. The General turned aside to speak to another officer. A captain hovered at Walters's elbow, then hurried off toward the bar. For probably the first time that night, the congressman stood alone and unattended.

"We're locked on target, Mol." Sam's murmur was a wash of warmth against her cheek. "Let's go get him."

They had taken only another step or two when a woman's voice floated across the night air.

"Major Henderson?"

Sam slowed, turned, muttered a curse under his breath. A vivacious young officer with an hourglass figure that even Mae West would have envied slid the patio doors shut behind her and crossed the flagstones. Molly didn't need an introduction to guess she was Lieutenant Donovitch of lip-lock fame.

"Captain Green told me you were here. I've been looking for you."

Realizing that she hadn't noticed Walters standing only a few yards away, Sam moved to intercept her. Before he could cut her off, she hurried into speech.

"I won't interrupt your evening. I just wanted to tell you I've been thinking about that matter we discussed the other day. I was stupid to let myself be intimidated. I'll go to the authorities, if you think it will help."

Although the lieutenant had lowered her voice, Molly's trained ear picked up every word. So, she saw on a swift indrawn breath, had Josh Walters.

He stood as if cast in stone, his eyes narrowed on Sam and the lieutenant. Suddenly, his gaze whipped to Molly. For an unguarded instant, his handsome mask slipped. She held his stare, her heart crashing like thunder against her ribs.

He knows!

He knows who I am, and now he knows that Sam's made a connection with Lieutenant Donovitch.

Maybe he knows that Kaplan's been asking questions, testing his alibi.

Molly realized she had to act quickly to capitalize on the drama of the moment. Gliding forward, she hooked her arm in Sam's.

"Darling, you promised to introduce me to Congressman Walters. He's right over there. You'll excuse us, won't you, lieutenant?"

The young woman gave Molly a surprised look, then turned a pasty white when she saw the man standing a few yards away. Without another word, she turned and hurried off.

By the time she and Sam stood face-to-face with Joshua Walters, Molly knew they'd missed their window of opportunity. The politician's mask had dropped back into place. His handsome face registered nothing but pleasure as he thrust out his hand.

"Sam! I told Jessie I thought I'd spotted you in the crowd earlier."

"Congressman."

"It's good to see you looking so fit...and in such delightful company."

If that smooth, educated voice hadn't raised the fine hairs on the back of Molly's neck, Walters's smile might have charmed her completely. It held just the right blend of polite inquiry and appreciation.

She didn't doubt that it got terrific results from the female half of the voting population. Sam made the necessary introductions, his voice low and deliberately neutral.

"This is Molly Duncan. Molly, this is our elected representative, Congressman Joshua Walters."

With one hand crooked in Sam's arm and the other firmly grasping her black evening bag, Molly neatly avoided any necessity of shaking hands with the man. Not only did she not want to touch him. She didn't want her damp palms to clue him into how nervous she was.

"Not my elected official," she replied coolly. "I haven't been here long enough to vote yet."

"Really?" Walters's blue eyes held hers with the ease of a consummate crowd handler. "What brought you to our wonderful state?"

He'd given her just the opening she needed. "A job, Congressman. I'm a translator and tour consultant with the Las Vegas Trade and Convention Center. I speak several languages, and have a good ear for accents" She tilted her head. "Yours, for example, caught my attention the first time I heard it." To her intense disappointment, he didn't rise to the bait.

"I'm not surprised. After a year or two at Harvard, this Wisconsin farm boy sounded strange, even to himself."

Dammit, she couldn't just come out and tell the bastard that he'd sounded more than strange the first time she'd heard him, he'd sounded calm and very,

very deadly. Desperately, Molly sought for some way to shake his composure, to startle him into saying something Kaplan and company would catch on their recorder.

The thought of the recorder triggered an idea. Detective Santos had said that technology hadn't advanced enough to record vocal signatures, but Josh Walters might not know that.

"You're right. Your accent is certainly distinctive. You'd be an excellent candidate for a voice print, using the Hammerstein-Taguchi methodology."

"I beg your pardon?"

Molly improvised wildly. "I studied linguistics before I decided to concentrate on spoken languages instead of the science of speech. One of the professors I studied with at the University of Tokyo helped develop the, uh, phonetic dimensions for vocal signatures."

The congressman's smile didn't lose its easy charm, but his eyes sharpened. So did Sam's. Ignoring the warning press of his arm against hers, Molly plunged ahead.

"Professor Taguchi demonstrated that some languages, like Japanese for instance, use only pitch to accent vowels and the consonants that surround them. Others, like English, use both pitch and loudness to create distinct speech patterns."

Dragging a quick breath, she played her bluff.

"Each voice forms its own, distinct signature. If someone familiar with the Hammerstein-Taguchi methodology had captured yours on a telephone recorder and matched it to, say, one of the campaign ads I recently saw on TV, I think you'd be surprised at the results. Very surprised.''

For the space of a single heartbeat, Molly thought she had him. Walters didn't so much as blink, but a sudden, swift stillness stripped some of the attractiveness from his smile.

Almost before she'd noted it, the stillness was gone. Moving with his customary grace, the congressman turned to accept a drink from the captain serving as his official escort.

''Thanks, Pete. Have you met Major Henderson and...Ms. Duncan, wasn't it?''

The bastard. Molly would have wagered her last dollar that her name had been emblazoned on his brain since the night he shot Joey the Horse. He wouldn't admit it now, though. He wouldn't admit anything. The curtain of intimacy surrounding them had ripped apart with the young captain's return.

''It's a pleasure to meet you, sir,'' he said, pumping Sam's hand. ''You, too, ma'am.''

Walters sipped the smoky scotch his escort had brought and watched the interchange with a casualness that grated on Molly's nerves like steel wool.

''I've just been selected for Test Pilot School,'' the captain confided to Sam eagerly. ''I know you hold the record for operational test hours in experimental aircraft, but maybe I'll blow it out of the skies one of these days.''

''Maybe you will.''

The General returned then, greeting Sam with a

slap on the back and Molly with a smile. When another couple drifted up, Sam took the opportunity to excuse himself and Molly. He waited until a wall separated them from Walters to spin her around. The easy smile he'd shared with the young captain and the General had disappeared. In its place was a fury all the more fierce for being tightly leashed.

"What in the hell were you doing?"

She didn't understand his anger. Neither did she appreciate it.

"Exactly what I came here to do—trying to shake your friend up a little."

"With that garbage about voice signatures?"

"Hey, he didn't know it was garbage."

"You'd better hope he did, Molly."

"Why? What the heck are you so uptight about, anyway?"

"You little fool. You deliberately gave him the impression you've got something on him. You didn't go to the police with it, so he probably thinks you're setting him up for blackmail."

"Well, I'm not, so..."

"You know that," Sam said savagely. "I know that. But Walters doesn't. If he didn't have a reason to silence you before, woman, you just handed him one on a silver platter."

Molly reared back. "I didn't mean... I didn't think..."

"That's obvious!"

She made up for that deficiency now. Her mind racing, she considered the consequences of her on-the-spot improvisation. None of them particularly appealed to her.

"Okay, maybe I got a little carried away."

"Carried away?" Sam gritted his teeth, controlling himself with an obvious effort. "Look, Walters might walk through that door at any moment. Let's find Kaplan and talk this through."

Clamping a hand around her elbow, he steered her through the crowd. They rendezvoused with Kaplan and retreated to the manager's office. Dee Santos joined them a few minutes later.

"That was some performance, Ms. Duncan," the detective said dryly. "You suckered me in for a while with that Hammerstein-Taguchi bit. Too bad you didn't pull in our target."

"How do we know she didn't?" Sam asked tersely.

Kaplan hitched a hip on the corner of the manager's desk. "You were there, Major. Do you think the congressman believed this voice patterning business?"

"If he did, he didn't show it."

"But we can't discount the possibility," the detective said slowly.

He rubbed his pendulous cheeks, thinking, considering, then turned a sober face to Molly.

"It might not be a bad idea for you stop by the station on the way home, Ms. Duncan. I'll get the supply folks to issue you one of our beepers. All you have to do is depress the button and it sends a silent, coded alarm to central dispatch."

That sounded pretty good to her. "We'll stop by."

"I wish we could dig up something concrete on the man," Kaplan muttered. "This business with the lieutenant bothers me, but…"

"She's here tonight," Sam informed him. "Walters overheard her say that she regretted letting herself be intimidated."

The detective's face brightened considerably. "She said that. Good. Point her out to me and I'll have a private chat with her. Maybe, just maybe, we'll get enough to convince the chief we should haul our congressman downtown for questioning."

When they returned to the ballroom, Sam and Molly both searched the crowd for the shapely young lieutenant. One of her friends informed Sam that she hadn't felt well and decided to slip away early. They relayed that message to Kaplan and got back to their table just as the president of the mess called the room to order. When the noise quieted, the program resumed.

After a lengthy and glowing introduction, Congressman Josh Walters took the podium to a rousing round of applause. Smiling, waving, joking, he finally silenced the room. Molly's skin prickled as the voice that had come to haunt her rolled across the ballroom.

Four hours later, the Mustang tooled through inky darkness, eating up the miles from downtown Vegas. Molly huddled in the passenger seat, fingering the small beeper Kaplan had given her while she chewed over the night's events. Josh Walters's charisma and powerful, passionate speech had added another troubling layer to her image of him as a murderer.

"He could be president," she murmured.

"Unless Kaplan comes up with some hard evidence, he will be."

The prospect made her feel ill. Rolling the beeper around and around in her palm, she let the past hour play and replay in her mind.

"He recognized me tonight, Sam. The moment he saw me with you, and you talking to Lieutenant Donovitch, he made the connection."

"Which makes your attempt to force his hand even more idiotic and dangerous."

Sam's knuckles whitened. He still hadn't worked out the tight knot that had formed in his gut when he saw Walters's glance whip from Pat Donovitch to Molly. Any doubt he might have harbored about the congressman's guilt vanished in that instant.

"I'm beginning to agree with you," Molly replied morosely. "I was tired of sitting back and waiting. I wanted to do something, to end this nerve-wracking, wait-and-see-what-happens game. Instead, I may have dug myself in deeper."

She let out a long, frustrated sigh and slumped down in the bucket seat.

"I pulled you into the hole with me, too, Sam. I'm sorry for that. If Walters gets away with murder, he's not going to forget that you were there with me tonight, or that you talked to Donovitch."

"Do I look worried?"

"Well...yes."

Deliberately, Sam unclenched his fists and forced himself to relax. He wouldn't help matters with any more reminders that Molly had upped the ante considerably tonight. He'd just make damn sure she didn't take a step without that beeper. He'd also make sure she didn't spend an hour alone in the foreseeable future. Davinia could help with that. Antonio, too. They could take the day shift. Sam would handle the nights.

He was debating how best to break it to Molly that she'd be on a short leash for the next few days when the Mustang's headlights picked up the sign for their exit. They left the interstate a moment later. Dark, silent houses and dimly lit shopping centers sped by, then the more developed areas fell behind. The road curved at an angle before cutting through an intersection and straightening for a long, deserted stretch.

It wouldn't remain deserted for long, Sam knew. Not at the rate civilization was eating up the desert. The huge, round concrete culverts waiting beside the road gave mute testimony to that. Earth movers had already chewed up trenches to swallow them. Then...

"Sam! Look out!"

He saw the slash of headlights coming at them from the right at the same instant Molly did. Recklessly, the driver had run the stop sign and now plowed through the intersection.

"He's not stopping!" Molly screeched, bracing both hands on the dash.

Sam wrenched the wheel. Tires screamed in protest. The Mustang skidded sideways. A dark sedan barreled right for them. At that moment, Sam had two alternatives. He could send the Mustang into a full spin and crash it into one of the cement culverts or let the passenger side take the impact of a collision with the oncoming car.

It wasn't a choice.

With the lightning reflexes of a test pilot, he floored the accelerator and spun the wheel full circle.

They almost made it.

The sedan shot by in a blaze of light and squealing brakes. The Mustang skidded in a full circle once, twice, with dizzying speed. Sam barely had time to throw himself sideways as far as his seat belt would allow, straining to protect Molly with his body, before metal slammed into concrete. He heard a sickening crunch. Felt his head slam back against the windshield. Saw the world go white, then black.

After the shattering crash, the sound of silence hit Molly with the force of a blow. She shook her head, dazed, disoriented, barely able to breathe from the weight pinning her to the bucket seat. Her neck ached. Her shoulder screamed where the seat belt had cut into it. When she shifted, slivers of broken glass dropped like confetti from her hair.

With her first, shuddering breath, the world finally stopped spinning. She pushed upright, grabbing at the body crushing down on hers.

"Sam! Oh, God, Sam!"

Sobbing, she scrabbled for a grip. More glass dropped, tinkling when it hit metal.

"Sam, are you all right? Sam!"

She levered him up enough to free one arm. Frantic, she flattened her fingers against the side of his neck and felt for a pulse. She wanted to weep with joy when she found it, beating strong and sure.

With a fervent prayer of thanks, she tried again to shift him. The prayer died on her lips when her hand came away wet with blood.

Fear shot through her once more, paralyzing her for a second or two. Then she groped for the release on the seat belt. It finally gave under her desperate pushing. As gently as she could, Molly scrambled out from under Sam's weight.

"Hang on," she said fiercely. "I can't reach your seat belt from here. The side's all crumpled in and mashed up against the concrete. I'll get you free, though. I promise. Hold on, okay? Just hold on."

Pleading, demanding, cajoling, she scrambled into the back seat and snaked her hand through twisted metal. Sharp edges sliced her skin. A ragged strip stabbed at her palm. It was then that she smelled gasoline. The fumes seeped up through the crumpled floorboards to sear her nostrils. Her heart stopped. All it would take was one spark, one scrape of metal on metal, to incinerate the Mustang and Sam with it. She had to get him out!

Panic choked her. Heedless of the sharp edges, she shoved her hand deeper. When she finally found the belt release, her fingers were so slick with blood that it took a half dozen tries to work it.

"Hang on, Sam. Please, please, hang on."

She scrambled out of the Mustang on the passenger side on all fours. Broken glass crunched under her. Her knee came down on a hard, square object. The pain didn't penetrate her mounting terror, but the shape of the object did. Grabbing it up with bloodied, trembling hands, Molly punched the button Kaplan had demonstrated what seemed like an eternity ago.

Praying that it worked, that Kaplan would send the closest patrol car speeding toward her development, Molly dropped the beeper and wrapped both hands around Sam's arm. She put everything she had into the pull. Her high-heeled sandals slipped in the slick, spreading gasoline. She landed on one hip. Glass and gas scored her skin. Flammable liquid soaked her dress. Disregarding both, she unbuckled the sandals and kicked them aside.

She was reaching for Sam's arm again when light stabbed the darkness. Molly sobbed with relief. The driver of the other car had come back!

A door thudded. Footsteps crunched on the roadway. Blinded by the bright headlights, Molly saw only a black silhouette.

"Help me!" she screamed. "He's too heavy! I can't move him."

She tugged on Sam's arm, expecting another pair of hands to appear beside hers. When they didn't, she threw a frantic plea at the still figure.

"Please! Help me! We've got to get him out!"

Through the frenzy of her panic for Sam, Molly heard the voice she could identify from the grave.

"On the contrary, Ms. Duncan. I think we'll leave him right where he is."

Chapter 14

Molly's nails dug into Sam's arm. Her throat clogged with horror. Crouching in the light of the other car's beams, she watched Josh Walters take two deliberate steps forward.

For a moment, his face formed a blur above the stark white of his shirtfront, pale and indistinct.

"You surprised me tonight, Ms. Duncan. I thought I was safe."

"I...I don't know what you're talking about," she bluffed desperately. "And I don't care. Just help me get Sam out. Please!"

In answer, he lifted his hand, and Molly saw the gun for the first time. It glinted evilly in the blinding beams, its barrel made hideously long and fat by the silencer.

"You can't shoot us, you bastard!" she cried,

abandoning all attempt at pretense. "You can't get away with murder again!"

"I don't have to shoot you," he ground out, his face flat with a terrible determination. "All I need to do is strike a spark, and both you and Sam will perish in the inferno caused by this tragic accident."

In the midst of her roiling panic, Molly felt Sam stir under her hands. She wanted to sob with relief, and scream with the fear that was spreading like the noxious fuel seeping all around her.

Then Walters raised the gun, and she knew with blinding certainty that she had only an instant to act. She had to get him away from Sam and the spreading fuel, and she had to do it now!

Releasing Sam, she surged up and around, twisting away from the beams thrown by the headlights, lunging for the entrance to the giant culvert only a few feet away. She heard Walters swear viciously, then the sound of his footsteps as he pounded after her.

Like a child in an oversize playground, Molly darted around and through the huge, concrete tubes, one after another, in a dizzying, zigzagging pattern. Her breath tore at her throat. The concrete shredded what was left of her stockings and scraped her elbows.

She plunged out of one dark tunnel and ran for the next. She heard a grunt behind her, another vicious curse. Suddenly, a flash of fire spit through the darkness. A bullet splatted into the concrete a few inches from her hand. Sharp concrete needles flew in all directions, slicing into her arm, her bare shoulder.

With a sob of sheer terror, Molly flung herself out of the culvert and made for the desert beyond.

It was darker here, away from the tilting headlights. The moon had disappeared behind scudding clouds. Tall saguaros threw black shadows across the rough, uneven terrain. There was an arroyo to the left, she knew, a gash in the earth that snaked its way toward the distant city. If she could find that in the darkness, she'd have the protection of the jutting angles. Walters couldn't risk letting her get away. He'd have to come after her, take her down, bring her back to incinerate beside Sam.

She'd lead him through half the desert first, Molly swore savagely, and straight into hell if she could.

She found the arroyo a second later, or it found her. Her foot came down on thin air. The rest of her followed. With a rattle of loose stones, she tumbled headlong to the rocky bottom. Molly sprawled there, stunned, while the moon slid out from behind the black clouds. She'd rolled to one side and had shoved herself up on one knee when she heard the pound of running feet. Instinctively, she flung herself to one side, hoping, praying the shadows would conceal her.

They didn't.

The footsteps slowed. Walters prowled the rim, silhouetted against the moon, listening, searching. Molly could tell the moment he spotted her. He froze, peered into the shallow depths. The gun leveled on Molly. She cringed back, curling into a small, tight ball.

"I didn't want this," he rasped. "I thought... I was sure..."

"You were sure you'd get away with murder."

"I didn't know you were a linguist," he bit out. "I missed that bit of information when I went through your house to find out just who I'd spoken to that night. You're the only link... The only one..."

The gun wavered. For a moment, Molly thought she had a hope. She played every card in her hand.

"If you kill Sam and me, the police will know it was you," she cried. "They were there tonight, at the club, watching you."

"I saw them," he snarled. "I've been keeping tabs on Al Kaplan and his so-called investigation since the night of...the night of the fund-raiser."

"You can't say it, can you? You can do it, but you can't say it. The night of the murder, Congressman. The night of the murder."

Desperately, she tried to buy time for Sam, for herself, for the police, praying for the sound of a siren in the distance, terrified Walters would hear it, too.

"How did you do it? How did you duck out of the gala and kill Joey Bennett?"

"I didn't duck out. My wife, the governor, half of Las Vegas will swear I was there the whole time."

"But you weren't."

"I was...except for the few minutes I went to take that phone call from the Speaker of the House."

"A phone call that lasted more than a few

minutes,'' Molly whispered. ''It lasted just long enough for you to slip away, kill Joey Bennett, and slip back.''

''No one in that mass of humanity would ever be able to say for sure.''

''The police can trace the call!''

He smiled then, a thin stretch of his lips that made Molly want to scream.

''It came right on schedule from the Speaker's office, Ms. Duncan. You don't think I'd leave something like that to chance, do you?''

''Why? Why did you kill him?''

The smile faltered. Something that might have been pain flashed across his face.

''I had to,'' he said with terrifying simplicity. ''As I have to kill you and Sam.''

The gun rose another few centimeters, centering on Molly. She wanted to uncoil, to gather her muscles for a final, desperate flight, but she knew it was hopeless even before Walters cocked the hammer back.

''I'm sor...''

A shadow lunged out of the darkness. Collided with Walters. The gun spit a ribbon of fire. Molly flung herself sideways just as dirt spouted from the arroyo wall mere inches from her face.

By the time she scrabbled out of the arroyo, Sam and Walters were rolling over and over, locked in a death grip. Even in the darkness, she could see the blood staining Sam's neck and shirtfront.

The gun spit again, a wild shot fired at the sky as

the two men grappled for the weapon. Frantically, Molly searched the rim of the arroyo until she found a heavy, flat rock. Gasping, snarling, feral in her need to help Sam, she brought it smashing down on Congressman Josh Walters's head.

"Sam!" She dropped to her knees between the still figures. "Oh, God! Are you all right?"

With her help, he pushed himself up on one knee, his face a mask of blood and agony.

"Get his...gun, Molly. I...can't see..."

She scrabbled in the dirt, her hands so shaky she almost couldn't pry the weapon from Walters's clenched fist.

"If he...moves, shoot...him."

"I will, Sam. I will."

"Kaplan... Wait for Kapl..."

His knee wavered, and Molly scrambled to break his fall as he toppled over. Sobbing, she dragged his head and shoulders into her lap. Holding the gun with one hand, she yanked Sam's shirttails out of his cummerbund with the other. With the wadded material pressed hard against his head to staunch the bleeding, she waited for Kaplan.

Molly had almost decided that she couldn't wait any longer, that she'd have to find something to tie Walters's hands and feet with and go in search of help, when she heard the cry of distant sirens. Relief speared through her, and she was sure she'd never seen anything or anyone as beautiful as the scowling,

heavy-jowled detective who came running out of the
night in answer to her cries for help.

After the eternity of waiting, it seemed like a matter of only a few more moments until an ambulance
arrived. Waving off the EMT who tried to treat her
bloodied hands and a cut on her face, Molly climbed
in beside the still unconscious Sam.

The ambulance took them to the Nellis hospital,
either because of Sam's uniform or because Kaplan
told them to. Molly didn't know and didn't care. All
that mattered to her was the smooth, practiced professionalism of the Emergency Room personnel
when the ambulance pulled into the dock and the
way the Air Force gathered to take care of one of its
own.

She was sitting in the ER waiting room, her hands
and face bandaged, when Rock and his wife appeared. The tall, lanky major had changed out of his
dress uniform into jeans and a navy sweatshirt with
the logo that Molly remembered from the yellow
T-shirt Sam had loaned her.

"We just heard about the accident!"

Gracefully awkward with her pregnancy, Peggy
dropped into the chair beside Molly and wrapped an
arm around her shoulders.

"Rock said the command post reported that Sam's
Mustang was totaled. Thank God you were able to
walk away."

"I didn't walk," Molly got out shakily. "I ran."

Before the startled couple could follow up on that
one, she turned to Rock.

"The ER physician came out a while ago and told me the preliminary X rays showed Sam fractured his skull, that he might require surgery."

He answered her unspoken plea with a tight nod. "I'll check out his status."

When he returned long moments later, his face was grim. "Evidently the back of Sam's head hit the windshield with enough force to crack both. He's being prepped now and will go into surgery as soon as the team's assembled."

Molly drew in a sharp, stabbing breath.

"We've got good docs here," Peg said, squeezing her shoulders. "Some of the best."

"This is the same team that treated Sam after he crashed through that malfunctioning canopy," Rock assured her. "None of us thought he'd pull through that accident, but he did. Drac Man's got a harder head than anyone I know, Molly. He'll pull through this one, too."

She wanted to believe him. She did believe him. But the thought that Sam might have to live with even worse pain than he'd endured for the past six months made her eyes burn with tears.

The next hours passed in a blur for Molly. Someone draped a hospital bathrobe over her shoulders, Rock she thought. She gathered it around herself gratefully. She'd washed as much of the blood from her face and arms and legs as possible and discarded her shredded panty hose, but large, rust-colored spots still stained her black dress. The medics had treated the cuts on her feet caused by the broken glass and her desperate flight across the desert. The green hospital slippers they'd given her matched the robe she now wore.

When Sam went into surgery, Molly, Rock and Peggy moved from the ER to a surgical waiting room done in soft, soothing desert colors. Peggy took advantage of the comfortable chairs to ease the strain on her back, but Rock paced and Molly stood at the windows, her arms wrapped tight around her, and watched as night flowed into dawn.

Reds, then golds, backlit the mountains to the east.

Worry, then a searing anger coursed through Molly.

Why hadn't she told Sam that she loved him? Why hadn't she admitted it sooner to herself? Why, why had she been so cautious, so damned determined to take things slowly, one step at a time?

Love was a risk, a prize to be snatched up and held onto for all it was worth. If... *When* Sam recovered, Molly vowed fiercely, she wouldn't let another sun set before telling him that she wanted to share more than a couch with him. She wanted to share Buck Randall and sweaty, steaming workouts and bucket seats and his house or her house or any place they decided to call home.

Slowly, the dawn brightened into day.

More people arrived. The General Molly had met briefly at the banquet. Another couple who greeted Peggy and Rock as old friends and Molly as new ones. Then Davinia and 'Tonio, after a phone call from Molly dragged them from sleep. She barely no-

ticed when the auburn-haired captain Sam had introduced her to last night showed up. Her striking
lavender eyes dark with concern, Janet Green huddled with Rock to learn Sam's condition.

He'd been in surgery for two hours when Al Kaplan arrived, red-eyed, unshaven and still wearing his
ruffled white dress shirt. He'd been on his way home
when he got the call from central dispatch, he told
Molly in a private aside. Rubbing a hand wearily
over his face, he filled her in on events subsequent
to Walters's arrest.

"The congressman gave us a full confession. He
admitted shooting Joey, but not for any of the reasons
we suspected. Seems his wife has a drug problem. A
serious problem. She almost OD'd last year, but the
MacGiver family physician covered it up."

"Oh, no!"

If worry for Sam hadn't drained Molly's store of
emotions, she might have felt a tug of sympathy for
the raven-haired woman who'd smiled and waved to
the audience so graciously last night.

"Evidently her dependency caused a rift in their
marriage that led the congressman to seek companionship elsewhere on occasion."

"Like with Lieutenant Donovitch."

Kaplan's shoulders lifted under his rumpled, ruffled shirt. "And one or two others, it seems. He
claims he loved his wife, though. Enough to try to
cut off her supply, anyway. Joey responded by threatening to expose the Missus's coke habit. Walters believed she couldn't take the public humiliation, and

he wouldn't let himself be blackmailed by the man he says was killing his wife by keeping her supplied with drugs.''

After facing Joshua Walters over the barrel of a gun, Molly didn't quite buy his story. She suspected that the man had been driven as much by his own political ambitions as concern for his wife's addiction. That would be for a jury to decide, though. Right now, her sole focus was the surgeon who walked into the waiting room.

Tugging a green surgical cap off his head, he glanced around the assembled crowd. He nodded to the General, but it was Molly he moved toward. Evidently he didn't have any difficulty identifying the woman wearing a green hospital bathrobe and a stark white face as the one he'd come in search of.

''Major Henderson sent me out to check on you, Ms. Duncan. He came out from under the anesthetic demanding to know how you're doing.''

''I'm fine,'' Molly gasped. ''What about Sam?''

The surgeon rubbed the back of his neck. ''The man's got the hardest head I ever took a saw to.''

When he saw that didn't exactly reassure the group, Molly in particular, he grinned.

''Major Henderson should be back in fighting form soon.''

''Thank God!''

A rumble of heartfelt relief rose from the gathered occupants of the waiting room. Never one to show her emotions, Molly nevertheless promptly burst into tears. The surgeon waited until she'd dragged up the lapel of the hospital bathrobe and swiped her nose before continuing.

"Sam sustained a fracture to his occipital...the bone that forms the floor and lower rear wall of the cranium. I had to go in and clean out some glass and bone fragments. It's a miracle none of them cut into the spinal column."

For a moment, nausea threatened to choke Molly. Sam had dragged himself out of the Mustang, followed her across a quarter mile of desert, and thrown himself at Walters with bone and glass grinding at the base of his skull. He could have severed his spine, paralyzed himself for life. She was still fighting down the taste of bile when she caught the tail end of the surgeon's next comment. Her fingers fisted on the bathrobe.

"What did you say?" she demanded, her chest squeezing. "What else did you find in there?"

"A bone fragment so small I almost missed it," he said slowly. "It was lodged right up against the edge of the foramen magnum...the opening the spinal column passes through...and didn't show on the X rays. The calcification makes me think the fragment's from an older injury."

Rock appeared at Molly's side and leveled a hard, hopeful look at the surgeon.

"What are you saying, Doc? Do you think this sliver of bone was left over from Drac Man's collision with that canopy?"

"That's my guess."

"Could that splinter of bone have caused his headaches these past months?"

"It could."

"And you got it out?"

At the surgeon's nod, Rock let out a joyous whoop. "Hot damn!"

Wrapping his arms around Molly's waist, he swung her in a wild arc and planted a kiss on her cheek before dropping her to attempt the same service for his pregnant wife. Laughing, Peggy settled for just a kiss. While the warriors in the room speculated joyfully about when Sam might return to full duty, Molly had more immediate concerns on her mind.

Like touching him.

And telling him she loved him.

And hustling him down to the nearest drive-through wedding chapel on the Strip, if he'd have her.

"Wh...?" She snuffled and took another swipe with the hospital bathrobe at tear-blurred eyes. "When can I see him?"

"Right now," the surgeon replied wryly. "Something tells me the Major won't let us take him into recovery until he sees you with his own eyes. Come on, we'll get you masked and gowned."

If she hadn't been hugging the surgeon's assurances that Sam should fully recover to her heart, Molly might have stopped breathing when she saw him lying on the gurney. As it was, she went decidedly weak at the knees. Bandages swathed his entire head, with only small holes for his eyes, nose and mouth. Bright crimson stained the gauze in spots, and he had so many IV lines and tubes strung from various parts of his body that she was afraid to get too close to him, let alone touch him.

Sam, however, had no such scruples. When he spotted her, he gave a low growl and lifted one hand an inch or so off the gurney.

"Mol…ly. You…okay?"

"Yes." She caught his hand in both of hers and clutched it against her breast. "All I got was a few scratches."

"More…than…a few."

"I'm okay, Sam, honestly. You just rest and get well quickly. We…" She sniffled behind her mask. "We still have to try out that couch you promised to share with me."

His fingers curled around hers with surprising strength for a man who'd just cracked his skull.

"More…than…couch. I love…you."

The tears poured down with a vengeance now. Of all the romantic settings they could have chosen for this moment, a surgical anteroom wasn't the one Molly would have picked.

"I love you, too, Sam."

Chapter 15

The sun blazed a bright arc across an achingly blue sky when Molly woke late in the afternoon. She rolled over in bed, wincing at the ache in her shoulder left over from the crash and let the sunshine pouring in through the windows bathe her in a healing balm.

She hadn't bothered to close the shades when Davinia and Antonio had brought her home just past noon. All she'd managed was a quick sponge bath, made awkward by the bandages on her scraped palms, and a mindless tumble into bed. The few hours of sleep she snatched had taken at least the top layer off her physical and emotional exhaustion.

She stretched languorously, ignoring the sharp stab in her shoulder from the pulled muscle. Despite her various aches, she felt wonderful. Terrific. Filled with the most incredible, delicious joy.

Smiling, she rolled over, dragging the puffy green duvet with her, and reached for the phone sitting atop its upturned cardboard box. Through eyes still sticky with sleep, she squinted at the number she'd scribbled down before leaving the hospital.

A man answered on the second ring.

"Hello."

Brimming with relief at the strong, sure tenor of Sam's sexy drawl, she smiled into the phone.

"Hello yourself."

She cradled the phone against her ear, tingling all over at the sound of his voice.

"I've been lying here thinking about you and what we'll do when you get home. As Buck would say, I've got a bad case of the wants for you, big guy."

A short silence answered her, then the drawl got even deeper.

"That's nice to know, sweetheart."

Molly frowned, catching a hint of an unfamiliar cadence in the reply. She pushed herself up on one elbow, her relief plummeting into worry. Sam must be in pain and trying to disguise it from her. Maybe his headaches had returned. Or the doc…

"Much as I'd like to work on that case of the wants," the speaker said laconically, breaking into her anxious thoughts, "I think you may want to speak to Sam. Hang on, he's right here."

Molly flopped back onto the bed, torn between laughter and mortification. Evidently, she'd just propositioned a complete stranger. She heard a short, pithy conversation, and what sounded like a roomful of males ribbing the helpless patient.

"Molly?"

"Who was that?" she choked out.

"My brother Jake."

"Oh, no!"

Sam's chuckle drifted over the phone. "Don't worry. Jake's too hog-tied by the sixty inches of pure energy he married to take you up on your offer, whatever the heck it was."

"I'll tell you what it was in person," Molly sputtered. "I'm never calling you again, by the way. Every time I do, I get the wrong man."

His reply was a slow, soft caress. "No, sweetheart, you've got the right man."

Her embarrassment melted, swept away by a rush of love. Sam was right. She had the right man, and she planned to keep him. Sam Henderson didn't know it yet, but she was going to hog-tie him every bit as tight as his brother reportedly was.

"Jake wants to meet you," he told her with another chuckle. "Marsh and Hoss, too. Reece says he doesn't need to. Any woman who can take down a killer like you did has his approval, sight unseen."

"Are all your brothers there?"

"Unfortunately. They're just getting ready to head up to my place, though. The doc says I need sleep more than I need four ugly faces hovering over me right now."

Gulping, Molly realized that she'd soon be facing

the four Henderson brothers. She had some serious repair work to do to her face and hair before that traumatic event.

"Get that sleep," she told Sam softly. "I'll see you tomorrow."

Facing the Henderson brothers turned out to be even more traumatic than Molly had anticipated.

Her doorbell rang less than an hour later. Smoothing her bandaged palms down the sides of the cherry red chenille top she wore with her jeans, she pulled in a deep breath and opened the door.

To a man, the Hendersons were tall and rangy and cast in the same ruggedly handsome mold as Sam. The oldest, Jake, did the honors, tipping his well-worn Stetson to the back of his head as he introduced himself and the others.

Molly showed them in, too overwhelmed by so much blatant masculinity to feel flustered by their quick, appraising glances around her near-empty rooms.

"Sam told us to make ourselves useful while he's stove up, Molly. Are you moving into his place, or do we move his stuff over here?"

She faced the semicircle, blinking. "I beg your pardon?"

"He said to move his stuff," the second brother, Hoss, put in with a grin. "Or your stuff. He wasn't particular which, as long as a certain couch got moved to the exact spot you want it."

"Oh, well..."

Faced with four handsome, shrewdly assessing males, Molly made a lightning decision.

"I don't have as much to move. We'll take my things over to his place."

"Sounds good to me," one of the men said, Reece she thought. "Just tell us when you're ready, and we'll start hauling."

"I guess that depends on when Sam gets out of the hospital."

"Or when you two plan to tie the knot," the fourth brother put in quietly.

Leaner, darker, more intent than the other three, he eyed Molly with a keen, slicing intelligence.

"Sam's had a rough time these past six months," he said slowly. "We knew it was bad when he stayed here to go through physical therapy instead of coming home to Arizona to recuperate. But we didn't know about the headaches...or about the fact that he was getting ready to hang up his uniform for good."

Jake shook his dark head, threaded with just a touch of silver at the temples. "If ever a man was born to fly, Sam was. He could take Pop's little Cessna apart and put it back together again by the time he was six."

"It must have cut him deep to face losing the Air Force. From what he's told us about you, Molly, it would cut him even deeper to lose you."

From the grim expressions on their faces, Molly got the impression that no one messed with a Henderson's heart and lived to tell about it.

"If you're asking whether my intentions toward

your brother are honorable," she replied, duplicating exactly their rich, rolling accents, "they are. As a matter of fact, Sam and I might hit the drive-by window at the Four Aces Casino and Wedding Chapel on his way home from the hospital."

Every one of the brothers blanched.

"I hope you'll reconsider that one," Jake pleaded. "Mom's the gentlest soul on earth, but I wouldn't want to be within a thousand miles of that woman if she misses her baby's wedding."

It took a mental leap for Molly to envision the six-feet-plus of solid muscle that was Sam Henderson as anyone's baby, but she managed. Barely.

"Why don't we all wait until Sam has a chance to vote on this?" she suggested.

For the first time, Reece's face relaxed. A smile every bit as wicked as Sam's tugged at his mouth.

"If we use Jake's marriage as a yardstick, I'd say that's the last vote Sam will have."

As it turned out, Molly and Sam weren't married at the Four Aces Casino and Wedding Chapel.

They were married at the Nellis chapel, with a weepy-eyed Davinia as maid of honor and four handsome Henderson men ranging beside their brother. Molly's heart swelled with pride at the sight of her groom, standing tall and straight in his dress uniform.

The medical board had returned him to full duty. Just last night, Sam had confessed that the need to drag on his flight suit and climb into a jet pulled at his very soul. But not, he'd whispered, his hands and mouth working magic on Molly, as much as he needed to make love to his green-eyed woman.

Those green eyes misty, she glided down the aisle to the strains of Buck Randall's ode to the slippery slide that was love.

* * * * *

invites you to go West to

Cameron, Utah

Margaret Watson's exhilarating new miniseries.

RODEO MAN...IM #873, August 1998: When ex-rodeo star Grady Farrell set eyes on his childhood sweetheart again, he vowed to put the past behind them. And then he met her—*his*—daughter...and decided to dust off those cowboy boots and stay forever.

FOR THE CHILDREN...IM #886, October 1998: Embittered agent Damien Kane was responsible for protecting beautiful Abby Markham and her twin nieces. But it was Abby who saved him, as she showed him the redeeming power of home and family.

And look for more titles in 1999—
only in Silhouette Intimate Moments!

Available at your favorite retail outlet.

B

COMING NEXT MONTH

#883 BRIDES OF THE NIGHT *Two outstanding stories in one irresistible volume

"TWILIGHT VOWS"—Maggie Shayne

Wings in the Night

Donovan O'Roark would do anything to keep another Sullivan woman from betraying the vampires of Dunkinny Castle. But when Rachel Sullivan filled the void in Donovan's soul, would he grant the beguiling virgin's request for eternal life—and love?

"MARRIED BY DAWN"—Marilyn Tracy

Vampire Gavin Deveroux *had* intended to eliminate vengeful Tara Michaels to safeguard his people. Then Gavin and Tara found themselves racing against time to be married by dawn. Were they destined to discover the greatest love of all?

#884 HARVARD'S EDUCATION—Suzanne Brockmann

Tall, Dark and Dangerous

Navy SEAL Harvard Becker was aghast when he was forced to work alongside alluring *female* agent PJ Rogers. To Harvard's amazement, his no-nonsense partner taught him a thing or two—on and off the field. Could it be that Harvard had finally met his match?

#885 HER COUNTERFEIT HUSBAND—Carla Cassidy

Mustang, Montana

Even before her heartless husband disappeared, Elena Richards knew their marriage was over. But now a decidedly different "Travis" was back—with amnesia!—and Elena was carrying his child. Could this marriage be saved?

#886 FOR THE CHILDREN—Margaret Watson

Cameron, Utah

FBI agent Damien Kane had pledged to protect Abby Markham and her twin nieces. But could he risk heartbreak again? Even if it meant offering the woman he loved a family of her very own?

#887 HIDING OUT AT THE CIRCLE C—Jill Shalvis

Way Out West

Frightened for her life, Haley Whitfield sought refuge on Cameron Reeves's ranch. Despite her tight-lipped secrecy, the laid-back, warmhearted cowboy offered her solace in his tender embrace. Could Cam convince Haley to trust him with her uncertain future?

#888 MOTIVE, MEANS...AND MARRIAGE?—Hilary Byrnes

Women To Watch

When Helen Stewart was assigned to prosecute her former lover for murder, she vowed not to succumb to her smouldering attraction for the sexy Irish cop. Yet when Patrick Monaghan swore his innocence, Helen knew she couldn't turn her back on the man she still desperately wanted.